FIVE-STAR STRANGER

FIVE-STAR STRANGER

A NOVEL

KAT TANG

SCRIBNER

New York   London   Toronto   Sydney   New Delhi

Scribner
An Imprint of Simon & Schuster, LLC
1230 Avenue of the Americas
New York, NY 10020

First Scribner hardcover edition August 2024

Scribner and design are trademarks of Simon & Schuster, LLC

Simon & Schuster: Celebrating 100 Years of Publishing in 2024

Interior design by Jaime Putorti

Manufactured in the United States of America

ISBN 978-1-6680-5014-9

For my parents, Jing Li and Jianshe Tang

FIVE-STAR STRANGER

CHAPTER 1

The first time Lily held my hand, she could only grasp my pinky and ring finger, and though she'd grown fast as knotweed over the years, at age nine she still gripped the same two fingers when we walked home from school together. Uncapped fire hydrants hosed down passing cars, making the September heat bearable as we side-stepped puddles and circumvented ladies carting sweet mangos sprinkled with Tajín. Lily wore a new tie-dye shirt we had made over the summer, though her skirt was beginning to fray around the hem. One thread in particular had unraveled enough to tickle her shin, and every couple of steps she would swat at it, as though it were a mosquito.

"Dad?" she said, her face turned up toward mine—inquisitive black eyes pinched down at the outer corners, giving her a serious look in line with her nature. I had been staring, perhaps too intently, at the thread, waving and dancing with each of her steps. I wanted to snip it or pull it, fix it, but instead I looked back to Lily with a smile.

"Yes, Moose?"

"Did you hear what I said?"

"Something about maps?"

"Yeah, Dad," she said, with an exasperated emphasis on the word *Dad* that took me by surprise. For as long as I'd known Lily she'd been a perfect daughter—perceptive, obedient, and smart—but also, especially around me, overly polite and presentable as though I might run away if I realized she was capable of being upset. This made sense: I saw her only once a week, so she always wanted to present the best version of herself, as though auditioning for a more permanent role in my life. So I didn't know whether to be delighted or distressed by her change in tone. "So, what I was saying," she continued, "was that the teacher told me I would make, like, a great cartographer because I have patience, you know? Most little kids—not that I'm little anymore because I'm almost ten—but, like, most kids don't have the patience to measure distances and make things to scale and that's so important because you can't have a toilet the same size as the kitchen!" I nodded along, wondering if I'd imagined the hitch in her voice earlier. After all, she still held on to my fingers, gripping a bit too tightly as she did whenever she was excited about an idea. It was this kind of involuntary earnestness that made me want to shield her from the evils of the world. But I could see the top of her head in closer detail every week as she shot up, and from this new vantage point it seemed only a matter of time before she saw the world not as I or her mother wanted her to, but as it really was.

We climbed the stairs of the eight-floor apartment building where Lily and her mother, Mari, lived. Their apartment was on the fifth floor and today, rather than playing the usual game of seeing how many steps she could skip at a time, Lily embarked on her new life as a cartographer. Last month it had been marine biology and we'd walked down to the Hudson River to peer disappointedly at the lifeless waters. It was a relief that a child's enthusiasm for the world was not so easily worn out, not even by the murk of a river steeped in city scum.

"I bet I could, like, make a map of this place!" Lily said, fingers tracing the dents in the stairwell walls where the edges of other tenants' tables and bed frames had dinged the plaster. "I don't think anyone in the whole world has made a map of all the cool stuff we've got like Mr. Ruiz's soup can collection and Henry's action figures and maybe we can even see the super's apartment in the basement, where he keeps his tools. What if there's even, like, trap doors and hidden passageways here too!"

"Why don't you start by mapping your room first?" I said, having had years of practice corralling peoples' exuberance.

"Okay, yeah, great idea!"

Rather than spending the afternoon working on her multiplication homework, we painstakingly drew a map of Lily's room, which was really just half of a bedroom, separated from her mother's side by a wide bookshelf. Their bedroom was even smaller than the room I'd shared with my mother after moving to New York City from Los Angeles at age seventeen, nearly a decade ago. Lily and I created symbols representing books and clothes and papers, making sure to mark exactly where they lay on the floor. When I asked what would happen when someone moved the toys, Lily narrowed her eyes as though assessing whether I was kidding, or if I really lacked some basic knowledge. Maps, she informed me, were always changing.

"The best they can hope to achieve is, like, a simulacrum that's useful and captures a moment in time. That's why cartographers will always have jobs."

I handed her a gray colored pencil to draw in the circle shape that represented Mr. Bunny, the single stuffed animal Lily owned.

I'd gotten her the toy cat years ago as a Christmas present, when she was too young to understand the difference between bunnies and cats. Mari had reimbursed me for the gift later that evening.

"You know what *simulacrum* means?" I said.

Lily added Mr. Bunny to her legend, which had its own page sprouting twenty-odd items and counting (pencils, plastic bags, expired coupons, candy wrappers, loose photographs of Lily and Mari, a Danish cookie tin full of receipts, a first-aid kit, a hand-sewn potpourri bag that Lily made in the first grade, etc.). She tugged at a pigtail, a little embarrassed to be caught using a word she didn't fully comprehend. "Not really," she admitted. "My teacher said it today, but she didn't really explain it. Do you know what it means?"

My experience with mapmaking was limited to the fourth grade when we spent weeks crayoning a map of the fifty states and then tried to hide our disappointment when the laminator bled the wax—Michigan's red mitt reaching down into the entire Midwest while the Southern states puked rainbows into the Gulf of Mexico.

"Dictionary?" I suggested.

"Yeah!" said Lily, jumping up to pull the dictionary from the shelf. "'Simulacrum,'" she read. "'Noun, a superficial likeness or representation of something.'"

"Hmm," I said.

"Hmm," said Lily, scratching her cheek as well. "Like how Mr. Bunny isn't a real cat."

"Right," I said. "Great example."

Lily, who was accustomed to praise from teachers and adults, beamed.

Around the time Lily began mapping the kitchen, which was differentiated from the living room by miniature tile-work drawn more meticulously by a nine-year-old's hand than had been laid down by the initial laborers, my phone buzzed. I ignored it until it buzzed again and again and again. I tried not to use my phone while with Lily, but worried that maybe Mari was caught up at work or that some other urgent issue had popped up, I snuck a quick glance.

The latest message, from the app and not from Mari, read, *Are we still on for 9pm dinner??*

Yes, I wrote back.

Don't forget the ring.

Of course, I replied, and turned my attention back to Lily, who was standing on tiptoes to see what I was looking at on my phone. She wasn't tall enough just yet.

"Is that Mom?" she asked.

"Sure is," I said, smoothing down her flyaway baby hairs. "She says she misses you."

"Let me see."

I slipped my phone into my pocket. "No can do, kiddo, private."

The Lily of two years ago wouldn't have even thought to ask to see my texts, and the Lily of last year might have asked but would have taken her father's response as absolute. Now, however, she seemed more aware of my little evasions. She crossed her arms, opening her mouth to say something but then biting down again—nervous, perhaps, to ask and find out that the answer would not be what she hoped. I took advantage of her hesitation by picking up a cream colored pencil. "I'll color in the kitchen tiles. You need to do math homework."

Lily gnawed on her lip a second longer and then silently plucked the cream-colored pencil from my fingers and handed me the burnt umber instead. For the rest of the afternoon, I scrubbed the kitchen floor with baking soda and vinegar until the tiles were ten shades lighter than burnt umber, though try as I might I couldn't clean them to a cream.

At 5:30 p.m., there was no Mari at the door complaining of a long day's work, beelining for the fridge to open a can of beer while trailing cigarette smoke. At 6 p.m., to distract Lily from her mother's absence, instead of preparing the usual family dinner, I heated up Chef Boyardee ("Is this a special day?" asked Lily). We ate canned pasta while watching the evening news from the couch rather than at the dining table. The recession was getting worse, another variant of COVID and the flu were going around, and politicians kept politicking. It was a year like any other, and eventually, I put Lily to bed. By then Mari was almost one hour late and I was cutting it dangerously close to my dinner. I paced the cleaned but sour-smelling tiles of the small kitchen, watching the minutes flip by on the microwave. A gentle 2 revealing an agitated 3, a workable 9 tumbling into an overbearing 10. Where was she? Was there an accident on the train? A shooting? An ambiguous medical emergency? What would become of Lily if her mother never came home? She was so much younger than I was when I had to navigate the world on my own.

Mari finally walked through the door at four minutes to nine, red from hairline to yellowed collar, her department store uniform crumpled where the blouse slipped out from her worn slacks. She reeked of gin and sweat.

"I'm so sorry," she said. "The new boss wanted to go out for drinks and wouldn't take no for an answer and my phone died and then the train was delayed because of, you know, typical MTA bullshit. Is Lily asleep already?"

I nodded. "She had a busy day."

"I'll pay for the overtime," Mari said, lowering her voice and pulling out her phone.

"Don't worry about it," I said, in a hurry to leave. "I'll see you next week."

Mari, cheeks flushed and graying baby hairs matted to her temples, shook her head. "No, no," she said. "No way." In all the years I'd known her, she had never been one to take charity despite sorely needing it. This brand of stubbornness reminded me of my mother, who believed asking someone else to do what you could do yourself was a sign of a useless human—a worthless sack of meat on earth.

"Here," said Mari, producing two crumpled twenties from the pocket of her faded jeans. I knew this was not an argument I could win, and starting one would delay me even further. So despite the fact that forty dollars could have bought Lily two new skirts that weren't unraveling, I accepted the money. It wasn't up to me how Mari conducted her finances or whether or not Lily had presentable clothes.

"Leftover pasta's in the fridge," was the only thing I said before slipping out the door. I took the steps down the stairwell two at a time.

CHAPTER 2

Dinner was a straight shot down the 1 train to the Upper West Side, where I rushed into the nearest department store, grabbing the best suit I could find in under a minute. As the cashier scanned the tags, I fixed my hair in the reflection of the sneeze guard. I pretended not to notice her sneaking glances my way. At six foot one, well built, and with vaguely Eurasian features, I'd been told by several people that I was "actually good looking," the "actually" undercutting the compliment as though it were an achievement for someone of my genetic makeup to be attractive. In the men's restroom I slipped out of my red flannel shirt and jeans and into the suit, whose pants were a touch short. Rolling up the bottom suggested a modern look in combination with the utilitarian boots I had on. There was no time to pick up a new pair of shoes. This was the best I could do given the time constraints and, truthfully, it wasn't half-bad. I shoved in any wayward tags and doused myself in Bvlgari Black on my way out.

The restaurant was standard New York City: unremarkably chic decor and a menu serving the melting pot of cultures we were told as kids we'd see in our neighborhoods but instead only found on overpriced plates. When I asked the hostess for Rachel Sherwin, she led me to the table where Rachel, in her late forties, wearing a powder-pink suit, her chestnut-colored hair styled in a tight chignon, sat fuming with great restraint.

"You're late!" she said through her teeth, and then pressed her knuckle to her lips as though surprised by the tone of her own voice. She tapped her lips a few times more, a nervous tic that left smudges of red on her fingers.

"Yes, my apologies," I said, resisting the urge to wipe the back of my neck with the cloth napkin. I tucked my feet away as she didn't seem the type to appreciate an unconventional ensemble, but she barely looked at me. By the strain in her neck and the way her eyes kept darting to the right, I could tell she was resisting looking behind her. I noticed nothing around us but more diners tucking into their cocktails and small plates of edamame hummus. I cleared my throat. "I was making sure I had the perfect, hum, gift for the evening," I said with a subtle wink and mischievous smile, a combination I'd practiced a hundred times to communicate just the right amount of we'reinthistogether-ness to someone you'd met for the first time ten seconds ago. This too she blew off as though I hadn't said anything at all, commencing to bite her knuckle again. Her nerves were understandable. Rather than telling her to relax, a patronizing command that encouraged the opposite result, I used the tried-and-true trick of distracting her hands with something to do and her mind with an easy line of questioning.

"Is he here?" I asked, nudging her half-drunk lychee martini closer to her hand.

"Yes," she said, snatching the glass by its stem and swirling the drink around. "In the corner by the orchids." She tilted her head slightly back and to her right.

"Is she with him?"

"That's her in the red. Gaudy."

I leaned to my left to peek behind Rachel while simultaneously motioning to the waiter. There was, indeed, an older man at the back corner table, maybe in his fifties, tall with a slightly crooked nose, wearing a nondescript slate-blue button-up, sitting side by side with a woman who looked quite a bit younger, black hair in a pixie cut, sporting a red dress with a dark crimson bustier, modesty only slightly preserved by the sheer sheen of an opalescent blouse.

"Do they always sit side by side like that?" I asked.

"It was my idea originally," said Rachel, sucking down her martini. "I told him that it could be fun if we sat next to each other and pretended like we were watching the theater of life. A dinner and a show every Thursday evening. I bet he uses that exact line on her."

The restaurant was three-quarters full, and there was no theatricality, yet.

"Are we ready to order?" said the waiter.

"Sure," I said. "The ravioli for me."

"That's what he does," Rachel continued with a sniff.

"Anything else?" said the waiter.

"Not at the moment, thank you."

"He takes credit for my brilliance."

"And for the lady?"

"Uses everything I've taught him on her."

"She'll have the cod."

"Very good, anything else to drink?"

The waiter lingered a moment longer and I could tell that he was an aspiring actor. He reminded me of the people my mother, an aspiring actress herself, had trained with: a little overeager for drama, attracted to the emotional epicenter of a room.

"Just water, thanks," I said. Though not trained as an actor myself, I knew how to play a supporting role. I'd spent enough time practicing lines with my mother to know how to gauge the moods of a tempestuous talent—which was why I was so good at my job. Never the star of any scene, I supported my clients as they acted out the drama of their own lives. And so I was able to recognize that Rachel, the top-billed actress of the evening, didn't care if I had anything to say. I was an emotional dartboard she could pin her confessions to. It was clear that she couldn't vent to her friends or family about her romantic troubles, so I sank comfortably into the role that most people didn't realize they truly wanted when they hired me—a nonjudgmental emotion receptacle: part therapist, part priest, part garbage bin. And indeed everything came up and out: the young woman by the man's side was not a post-divorce girlfriend as I'd expected, but rather his baby-faced wife. And also, according to Rachel, a witch. "You don't look like that in your early fifties without sacrificing *something*, if you catch my drift." And then, after taking a small bite of her miso cod, "She's a Gemini, so." When she finally gave in and took a peek behind her, I locked eyes with the man for a second before he looked down and diligently attacked his steak with fork and knife.

By the time I finished my entrée of lobster ravioli smothered in a peri-peri-infused cream sauce, I had to ask the obvious.

"So why the ring?"

"Well," she said, licking her teeth, "I've been thinking on this for a few months now, ever since our affair started." Though most people were ashamed to use the word *affair*, Rachel emphasized it as though it were capitalized, and in the crook of her smile I saw that she took some pride in being the other woman. Perhaps it made her feel powerful. Because even though this man's wife wasn't the one spending long minutes studying her reflection in the mirror—smoothing out the wrinkles that had moved in over the years and settled permanently between her brows, lifting her cheeks and letting them fall, lift and fall—her husband still desired Rachel, who did bear the signs of aging. She patted down the sides of her chignon, though not a strand was out of place. "And I've come to the conclusion that he hasn't decided to leave her yet because he feels no sense of urgency. Perhaps he thinks I'm too old for another man to marry. Or maybe he believes that I haven't gotten over my late husband, bless his soul. But five years is ample time to grieve, wouldn't you say?"

The extra button attached to the price tag of my suit itched my back and I shuffled a bit, which Rachel took as confirmation.

"So anyway, your proposal will show him that I'm in my prime and very marriable."

"And you'll prove that by marrying someone else?"

"No, by being proposed to by someone else, and turning them down."

Rachel's initial message about the job had mentioned a proposal, and I had faked enough of those that there wasn't much to prepare—the only step necessary had been hitting up my ring resizer because her ring size was slightly smaller than the last person I'd proposed to. There hadn't been any mention of a rejection.

"You're turning me down?"

I had no problem being rejected; I knew better than to let personal feelings or ego get in the way of my work. In fact, many of my gigs were practice breakups or public rejections by people who wished to be seen as more desirable to those around them—I was thrown not by the notion of being turned down but by the logistical reality that rejection required more preparation on my end (a wig, a prosthetic nose, even glasses) to hide my identity. Humiliation, rather than celebration, was so much more gossip-worthy to strangers. Whereas a successful proposal was a story for diners to, at most, offhandedly tell their friends, a rejected proposal was a tragicomedy that could make the rounds on the internet, with my real face on display. My job required anonymity if I wanted future clients who wouldn't take one look at me and ask if I wasn't the guy whose proposal got rejected by the old woman in a power suit. I could not be made into a meme.

"Is that a problem?" Rachel asked.

"Dessert menu?" said the waiter. This man had caught wind of conflict in the air emanating from table twelve and was drawn to it, like a fruit fly to rot. It was both impressive and annoying.

"Sure . . ." I said, then turning back to Rachel, "and no. No problem at all, your happiness is my happiness." If I had a motto, this would be it: your happiness is my happiness, my guiding principle, my mission statement.

I noticed a server approach the couple's table and leave with the check holder, a hollowed-out book with the carved pages glued together to make a box. "I think they're about to leave," I said.

"Do it now!" Rachel said, biting her knuckle so hard I was afraid she'd draw blood.

"Excuse me," I said to the waiter, who was still holding the dessert menus and seemed to have forgotten his job to pass them over. "Could you please stand over here?" I pointed to a spot on the floor that blocked the other diners' view of my face. He, excited to be a part of something, and accustomed to stage direction, obliged. When I got down on one knee, Rachel stood stone-faced while the waiter squealed in delight, and I noticed the man and his wife at the corner table looking our way. The man, who had been rushing through his meal all evening to avoid a run-in with his mistress, looked miserable at this development while the wife beamed, saying something that I couldn't quite make out about "theater."

I cleared my throat, launching into a speech I'd given dozens of times though with a few modifications from Ms. Sherwin. "Ever since I first saw you, I knew you would be an incredible life partner. You are truly one in a million, and I would be foolish to let you go. Will you, Rachel Sherwin, make me the happiest man on earth?"

A flash came on nearby and I wedged myself further behind the waiter's, luckily ample, thighs. I had a clear view of the man at the corner table, who was now whispering into his wife's ear while rubbing his temple, no doubt trying to escape this third act, but his wife would have none of it. She was enthralled by romance, something that he, likely, was not providing her with enough of these days.

"Well?" prompted the waiter.

I nodded toward Rachel to indicate that yes, indeed, her lover had seen this mock proposal unfold.

"I can't!" she said, a bit too loudly if anyone asked me, though, of course, no one would. "I'm in love with someone else." At this, she turned around just in time to see the man slip away into the bathroom. His wife was busy either texting her friends or posting for internet denizens what she had just witnessed. I grabbed a dessert menu and sat down, hiding my face as the waiter murmured "I'm so sorry, man." And with that, the charade was over as suddenly as though a director had called cut. I could sense the sidelong glances of other diners trying to rubberneck at my humiliation, no doubt satisfied that as poorly as their day was going, at least it was far better than mine. In this I was satisfied: not only was I able to perform for Rachel, I'd also offered the fine diners of this Upper West Side establishment a little bit of perspective on their lives. I propped the menu up as a divider, pretending to engage in a heated discussion with Rachel as she received a slew of texts that she seemed quite proud of.

"He's livid!" she said.

"Wonderful." My phone in my pocket buzzed, indicating that the allocated hour and a half was up. "Have my services been satisfactory?"

"Oh yes," she said. "Perfect."

"Perfect. Please leave a five-star review."

"Oh sure," she said, "why not."

"Thank you." I pretended to drop my napkin and bent down to slide on the face mask I always had on hand for a quick disguise like a reverse Clark Kent. It is amazing how unrecognizable one can become simply by obscuring the nose and mouth. "Enjoy the rest of your evening and thanks for using Rental Stranger."

By 10:30 p.m., the department stores had already closed, so I would have to return my suit with its attached tags tomorrow. A payment from the app came through with a note that the client had given a five-star rating and a 25 percent tip. Happy that she was happy, I whistled a nameless tune as I rode the subway home. Years ago, when I first started in this business, I might have had moral qualms about helping someone meddle in another's marriage, but I soon realized that differentiating between those who deceived and those who didn't was futile. The latter didn't exist. So who was I to judge these shades of moral gray? Who was I to say who deserved help in achieving happiness and who didn't? As long as it was legal and as long as they paid me, I would do my job to the best of my ability.

Every Rental Stranger on the app had their own way of doing things; the company didn't care how you conducted your business so long as you kept getting good reviews and didn't land them in any legal trouble (and anyway, I was sure we had signed away all liability on their part). My rules were simple but absolute: I would (1) form no emotional attachments, (2) participate in no illegal activities, and (3) allow for no touching beyond a hug or holding hands. My high ratings on the app spoke for themselves.

On a bleak stretch of Canal Street, where more shop fronts were shuttered than open, I strolled up to my building entrance—an unmarked metal door that was only distinguishable by the small call box graffitied over with yellow paint. I wasn't sure what this building was once used for, but even now it smelled like burnt rubber on hot days.

At the entrance, I fist-bumped a couple of the African immigrants who hung out on the street selling everything from Cucci bags to LSD. "Nice date?" asked the tall one with a ten-thousand-dollar watch (real, he assured me) on his wrist. I never asked his name and he never asked mine.

"Yeah," I said. "Went well."

He looked me over and tapped near his collarbone. "It's about the peak lapels now though."

"You know," said one of the other guys, with a lazy eye, "I have a perfect watch to match your suit."

"Or cuff links," a third guy said, chewing on the end of a blunt.

"How's business going?" I asked.

"Slow," said the tall one. At night, the sidewalks all but emptied out. Even the Asian aunties hawking their designer-ish bags were gone. Only the chatter of these men, the occasional lost SoHo influencer, and cars rolling past on their way to Jersey City populated this corner of the city.

"Better luck tomorrow," I said.

The tall guy tapped his chest again. "Peak lapels."

"Thanks," I said. "I'll keep that in mind."

The narrow stairwell of my building allowed only one person to pass at a time, but oddly, in my near decade of living there, I'd never run into another tenant. I did, however, hear people walking by my door from time to time, and four years ago my elderly upstairs neighbor died in his bathtub and my walls wept with the overflowing water. Since then I no longer hung my hat collection on the wall and instead kept the hats on two hat racks, wigs in three large plastic bins, shoes in stacked cardboard boxes, clothes on several rolling racks, glasses and other accessories on a shelf, plus hamperfuls of scarves, belts, suspenders, bandannas, shirt stays, and socks. If anyone were to enter my apartment, their first thought would be "hoarder" and their second would be concocting an excuse to turn right around and head back down the narrow gullet of a stairwell. Luckily, no one ever visited my small studio, where walking paths were tight and convoluted as ant tunnels, and I had to move a stack of books back and forth to access either the refrigerator or the cupboard. Despite the mess, the apartment wasn't dirty—my mother instilled in me a love of cleanliness worthy of zealots. It was an organized clutter, this space that was part storage room, part office, and part living area. As the proportions showed, I didn't require much of the latter.

In front of my cracked bathroom mirror I brushed my teeth, seeing and not seeing my own reflection, checking it as one would a product. Did it need a shave? A haircut? Were there blemishes that I could prophylactically take care of? Did this smile still ooze charm and this furrowed brow indicate appropriate gravitas? After making sure everything was in order, I wiped down the sink and mirror, showered, and got into bed. Some days required practice or supplemental reading for a part, but now that I'd been working nearly a decade, most roles required little preparation and I could pack my day full of client work. I checked the app to see who I was meeting up with tomorrow, responded to a few new inquiries, and scrolled through the day's news. I watched half a dozen videos on fixing loose threads and unraveling hems. No one asked me how my day was and no one wished me a good night. I closed my eyes and traced, in my mind, the metro lines and bus routes of the city until I fell asleep with the lights still on. I was, embarrassingly, afraid of the dark.

CHAPTER 3

In the mornings, diffuse natural sunlight filtered into my apartment through windows I'd papered with takeout menus (efficiently ensuring my privacy and also expediting the process of choosing what to eat). As always, my overhead light was on when I woke up to start my daily routine. First, a release of morning stiffness guided by my right hand, with a visual assist from the round ceiling light with the stud like a nipple in the middle. The focus of my libido over the years had become this tit of light; I tried not to psychoanalyze that one. Mostly it was quick and efficient and it cleared my head for the rest of the day. Next was grinding coffee and toasting a bagel from my freezer. The tiny kitchenette had two burners, which was one more than necessary for its singular purpose: boiling a small pot of water. Next came calisthenics (fifty push-ups, fifty crunches, fifty squats), then finally, the most important part of my morning: the bowel movement. Getting this out of the way at home was critical since I really couldn't shit on my client's dime, and fouling up someone else's bathroom destroyed the illusion of a perfect husband, boyfriend, in-law, what have you.

It was a tough job regulating your GI tract, but I was a compulsive perfectionist, just like my mother.

My first gig of the day was a coffee date in Williamsburg with a young woman who had requested a mid-thirties professor. I assumed she had the hots for a classics prof, so I spent my morning brushing up on phalanxes and declensions. Though in the end what she'd actually wanted was for someone to tell her that she'd made the right choice in entering her program, that she was talented, and that she should keep going, despite evidence to the contrary. I told her all of that and more, and in return received a handsome sum and a five-star review. In the afternoon I walked with a couple around Central Park and joined them for dinner, politely declining their invitation to drinks at their hotel afterward as it was not a part of the assignment. When evening fell, I made my way to Stone Street in the Financial District to join an aging banker who'd hired me to play an intern in my early twenties. This required a quick pit stop at my apartment (my back-stage changing room in this city) as there had been a beauty to the art of shedding ten years over the course of a day: scruff and dark circles (eyeshadow) in the morning, and clean-shaven with acne (prosthetic) in the evening. Makeup, now a staple in my daily work, had been a tricky aspect for me for a long time. I couldn't walk up to makeup counters and ask for assistance without receiving questioning looks from patrons and employees. Luckily, the internet was now overrun with makeup tutorials, and with a few months' practice I could strobe and stipple like the best of them. It helped that I had inherited my mother's smooth skin, strong bone structure, and eyes that refused to water. I assumed my wild brows, which I was constantly plucking, came from my father—but I'd never known the man.

On the intake form, the banker's name was spelled Ajay, a quick YouTube search confirming that the proper pronunciation was akin to what one might say when spotting the blue bird of spring. But when he introduced himself it was as A.J., two harsh letters with no lilt. Truthfully, I could sympathize. My name was also abnormal and I imagined that ever since preschool, when his teacher looked at this configuration of letters and said "A.J.?" the tracks of his life shifted and his future as a finance bro was inevitable. But who could blame him for adopting an anglicized moniker? Back in his day there were no Mihirs, no Anushkas, no Rahuls, only Bens and Beckys. It wasn't until later in life, when America began to embrace (or at least coolly shake hands with) the Jings and Josés of its national rosters, that Ajay ever encountered people pronouncing his name the way his parents did. By then, it must've sounded like an obnoxious hurdle in the frat-to-finance track he'd been barreling down his whole life. "It's A.J.," he would tell them, indignant and impatient as the clerk who'd taken down my mother's birthplace at the DMV. "You mean HANGzhou?" they'd said, full of authority while strangling the Mandarin like a noose around the neck.

Ajay, wearing a fleece vest and long-sleeved dress shirt despite the warm weather, ordered beers for the both of us as we sat at a wooden picnic table on Stone Street beneath strings of Irish flags. "I've never done this before," he said. "Paid for a *dude's* company. Are you like the people in those movies?"

"No," I said. I knew the movies he was talking about and had been thoroughly disgusted when I'd seen them (for research purposes). Unlike those doe-eyed noobs, I wasn't working this job to slip n' slide my way into true love or fulfill some weird fetish—as though those were the only reasons to be a rental! It didn't take much imagination to comprehend why I did what I did day in and day out. After all, why did a master chef slave over perfectly poached duck breasts or neurosurgeons offer up their twenties and thirties to practicing temporal lobectomies? Because they were good at it, it paid the bills, and it was a net positive in the world. My profession, of course, was less mainstream and less lauded. I could never brag about my accomplishments. Despite—or perhaps because of—the way I could make them feel, I sensed that some of my clients were ashamed of using my services and I would never do anything to jeopardize their reputations. To preserve anonymity, the selections page of the app did not feature any photos—only rankings and reviews. After the initial inquiry, a photo could be requested.

"It's still fucking weird," Ajay said.

I smiled good-naturedly and shrugged. I could have said, You're the one who hired me, or We're all paying for company somehow, but I knew that wasn't what Ajay wanted to hear. Those who hired me were lonely even if they spent their days surrounded by others, and though Rental Strangers were, by now, a well-known aspect of society, rarely did anyone suspect that we were at the party. Even those who hired us liked to pretend they were somehow above exactly what they were doing; I found it was best to let them express their mental discordance however suited them, and in the case of some clients (men especially) it was through insulting me. So be it.

"Whatever," said Ajay, his depth of introspection so shallow I could walk through it and not get wet. "We'll see if you're worth it. Drink up."

I drank my beer without complaint. Drinking on the job was not against my rules, so long as I didn't get drunk.

"You good at picking up chicks?" said Ajay. But before I could answer, he (who had been some sort of lady's man in his prime) turned our table on Stone Street into a war room: the shots he ordered and downed in succession represented women, we were the beer steins, and the schmucks we would outdick were salt and pepper shakers. Battle tactics were replete with jargon like *approach priming, negging, IOIs, IODs, save-me eyes, AMOGing, DHV*, and so on. "So here's where you come in," he said, pushing my stein forward. "You're the vanguard." Or maybe he didn't say *vanguard*, but I knew that's what he meant. "Girls see someone my age and they think 'creep'—I know, it's fucked, but women, right? All they see is what's out here, they don't see what's on the inside"—he took a long pull of beer, burped—"of the wallet, and the pants, haha, know what I mean? Anyway, they see someone young and handsome like you— pop that pimple, would you? It's gonna throw off our game—and they'll be willing to parlay while I buy a couple rounds of drinks. Obviously top shelf, and then they'll welcome me with open arms and hopefully"—he winked—"legs."

At one time, Ajay must have cut a striking figure, a commanding general with steely gray eyes and an aquiline nose, but now in his mid-fifties his features were buried in the doughiness of a face that met the lip of a beer bottle several times a day and his bronze coloration mottled with the patina of inevitable cirrhosis.

At the door to the club, Ajay slipped the bouncer a hundred, and they bumped fists like best friends. I could have judged, but the bouncer and I were kindred spirits—we were both being paid by this old man for something only money could get him, and so what? After working these long years, didn't he deserve what the fruits of his labor could buy? At the table, Ajay ordered two bottles of Grey Goose, which were promptly paraded to our table by voluptuous women batoning Roman candles. A silver platter of fruits also appeared, and I wondered if the satyrs feeding us grapes and servants waving palm fronds weren't far behind.

"Remember everything I taught you?" said Ajay, pinching and rolling a blueberry between his fingers.

25

"Sure do."

"Okay, Zeke, go get 'em."

Zeke was the name Ajay had chosen for me. I always asked my clients to name me—you could tell a lot about what they wanted based on the name they chose. Zekes, according to Ajay, were openers not closers.

Drink in hand and battle map in mind, I ignored all of Ajay's advice and did what I always did at clubs: smile, introduce myself, ask if she wanted a drink. Women were often pleasantly surprised by a proper introduction—though the name I gave was always fake—and I'm sure my looks had a little something to do with my success rate.

Ajay crossed his arms as I brought a group of women over. "Too old!" he hissed in my ear. I supposed I had shown my own preferences by choosing these women, world-weary and a bit wild. I recalibrated my vision to see the club as Zeke or Ajay would see it—their sacrosanct spaces, temples where the devoted gathered to ritualistically lose their minds and their bodies to the beat and the drinks and the pills. The spiritual leader spun tracks on a stage and occasionally instructed his followers to worship with their hands in the air as acolytes performed on poles. After apologetically pouring the older women a shot and sending them on their way—they were too proud and all too aware of their lined necks to make a fuss—I looked for a woman in the crowd who would fit Ajay's definition of hotness: someone who hadn't suffered more than a bachelor's degree. It wasn't difficult; the club was full of them.

This time, when I introduced two girls to him, Ajay smiled and in his satisfaction he looked almost handsome. He took a particular shine to the redhead, whose hair touched the small of her back, and tasked me with keeping her friend occupied: a Korean American, Rina, who had just begun working in the city. Our conversation, as most New York conversations go, revolved around what we did, where we lived, and where we ate. To all three of those points, I lied.

"Why are you hanging out with, like, an old man?" said Rina.

"He's one of my bosses," I said. The first non-lie of the evening.

"Ooohh in banking? Is he, like, rich or something?"

"Yes," I said, though how rich I did not know. "Very."

Rina nudged her friend and the two of them conferred, sweaty temples pressed together as a slow smile spread over the redhead's face.

She flounced back to Ajay. "Do you guys wanna get out of here and go to, like, Death and Co or something?"

It was so earnest—this desire to use Ajay's money to cross off going to a speakeasy from their New York bucket list—that I nearly laughed.

"I can do you one better," said Ajay, pouring a round of vodka for the table. "Do you know Pappy Van Winkle?"

"Where's that?" asked Rina.

"I'll get a car," said Ajay. "Let's get out of here."

When we reached the entrance of an apartment lobby and the doorman held the glass door open for us, I could sense Rina's hesitation.

"If you're tired—" I offered, but Ajay cut me off.

"Don't be lame, Zeke," he said. "It's Friday. I'll give you Saturday morning off, that's how generous of a boss I am."

I had a client Saturday at ten a.m., but Ajay had rented me until two in the morning and it was only just past one—so I followed him and the girls into the elevator. Nothing illegal was happening; I wasn't breaking any of my rules. Rina asked if the bar was in this building. Ajay didn't answer. Instead, as we rode up the pencil tower, Ajay rattled off names of the A-list celebrities and moguls who lived in his building, each flashing number occupied by another star like a constellation in a thirty-four-floor line, and the girls were placated like nothing bad could happen in the presence of such success. The elevator opened up to the foyer of Ajay's bachelor pad, where his immense shoe collection lined the wall. The two girls glanced at each other. I fiddled with my cuff, giving the appropriate appreciative nod, like I was accustomed to this level of wealth displayed in footwear, and that turning your entryway into the museum of Balenciaga kicks and Gucci slides was the height of class. While Ajay gave a tour of his apartment, I couldn't help but notice that adjacent to the light of wealth were the shadows of a solitary life: a marble-topped kitchen with the latest gadgets (a trash can full of takeout containers and candy wrappers), a bathtub big enough for four people and a separate shower/steam room with double showerheads (a cup with a single toothbrush, its bristles splayed out like a skirt), floor-to-ceiling windows in the impeccably decorated living room overlooking Madison Square Park (a worn imprint in only one seat of the couch).

As it turned out, Pappy's was not at all like the sports bar in LA with the same name that my high school friends and I would sneak into to get drunk off of five-dollar Bud Lights, but rather a five-thousand-dollar bottle of bourbon that Ajay splashed nonchalantly into our glasses, Rina and I receiving noticeably less. This was fine by me since I don't have a taste for rare liquors and I was reaching my limit drinks-wise (an unofficial rule: five drinks in a night). But when Ajay was stingy with Rina's refill as well, she gripped her friend's hand tightly and declared that it was time for *both* of them to get going. "Oh come on," said Ajay, unable to hide the irritation in his voice. "We're just getting started." He caught himself, and then, a bit softer, coaxing, "I have extra bedrooms if you want to crash."

"It's almost two," I said.

"Bathroom?" said Ajay, standing up. "I'll show you where it is." Out of earshot of the girls, Ajay gripped my arm, his thickly padded fingers digging into my skin. "C'mon, man, this is the perfect setup. You stay and bang the Asian chick and I get my jollies too. Win-win."

"It's almost two," I said again, like he hadn't heard me the first time. "This is the end of my assignment."

"What, you want to get paid more?" said Ajay. "I can give you a grand to stay the night, and all you have to do is bang some busted girl. I mean, just turn the lights off if it's so bad."

"She's not ugly."

"Then what is it?" he said. And then, releasing my arm with a recoil, "Are you gay?"

"No," I said.

"Well, what is it, then?"

What was it? Besides a growing distaste for this pushy, fleshy man, my mother had drummed into me the idea that sex was vile. Before cracking open any novel or script, she would have me read it first to check for sex scenes. Sometimes, on account of being too young, I would miss the metaphors of coitus, and my mother would stop her reading and meticulously rip the pages at the point just before two bodies became one. "Reread it," she would say. "Isn't it better this way? The tension richer? The characters far more interesting? Sex"—and she said the word without emphasis, so emotionless she could have been talking about taking out the trash—"is the lowest common denominator. It is not worthy of art or literature. I will not tolerate it, you hear me?" And she, true to her word, refused to play any roles fixated on romance. But much to her dismay, leading ladies were always in love, or being loved, or searching for love, and so my mother mostly took on roles as extras: nonspeaking parts where her goal was to serve the heroine a drink on a tray without spilling it down her shirt, unless, of course, spilling it down her shirt was exactly what was needed so that the leading lady could reveal the lace edges of her lingerie to the leading man across the table. And though I wholeheartedly agreed with my mother's literary tastes, I'd secretly and shamefully ferreted away the shorn halves of these books, rereading the scenes that made my heart beat staccato, and which on a few occasions resulted in me waking up in the middle of the night, encased in sticky boxers that I ran furtively under the tap, worried sick that my mother would find out about my transgressive desires. If only I'd kept these urges hidden. If only I'd listened to my mother.

"It's against the rules," I said. And then, "I'm sorry, I need to go."

"Fucking pussy," said Ajay as I turned toward the elevator.

The irony of that insult, it seemed, was lost on him. But it was what he'd wanted, wasn't it, naming me Zeke—an opener, not a closer.

It wasn't that I was asexual—no, even now my desires remained, ballooning in my mind, pressing against my temples, squeaking in my ears. Only, now I knew how to puncture the lust. It wasn't difficult, for the thought of a part of me disappearing into another person was enough to make my body numb and my breath shorten, and I had to dig my nail into my thumb to feel my own flesh again. I wasn't seeking that kind of annihilation.

As the elevator doors closed behind me, I felt a twinge of regret—not for the lost potential of physical intimacy, or for leaving these two tipsy women alone with a wolfish man (though the way Rina had gripped her friend's hand made my chest ache; but so what, they were adults and could make their own choices even if they were bad ones—I wasn't their father), and not even for the potential loss of a thousand dollars (I wasn't, nor did I want to become, familiar with New York's prostitution laws). No, I was a professional, and my one regret was that though I'd performed my job perfectly, I knew Ajay was unhappy with the result. I hoped that his review of me would be fair.

CHAPTER 4

Ajay's one-star review was anything but fair, but it was also outrageous and homophobic enough that I flagged it for the Rental Stranger screeners and hoped they would remove it. I needed to preserve my five-star reputation. Bad reviews, in our industry, were lethal. Because of the potential for abuse on a platform where anyone could sign up to be a Rental Stranger, the company took poor reviews seriously and kicked off any rental who received successive one-star reviews. I'd seen it happen countless times: one day a rental was rising in the ranks, and the next, gone. Of the top-ranked handles, mine was the only one that had remained consistent for the last five years. Once I entered the top tier, I never faltered—and I had a five-year gold star badge to prove it (my inbox doubled in inquiries after this status bump). I credited my success to a steadfast adherence to my rules and a refund to those who were less than satisfied, which was luckily a rare occurrence. In this case, a refund wasn't necessary—instead, I wrote a note to the company explaining last night's situation. Ajay was a first-time user, and I had been on the app for nearly a decade, and a top-rated rental for half that time; in a he-said-he-said scenario I hoped that this was a no-brainer.

After completing my morning routine, I changed into a faded Ramones T-shirt, baggy jeans, glasses, and a black shoulder-length wig. At each subway station, when I had a few seconds of internet, I refreshed the app, but the single-star review remained. The man sitting next to me was similarly refreshing his browser at every stop, reading a few pages more of hentai at a time. I put my phone in my pocket and looked straight ahead.

At a wine bar in the West Village, with its windows thrown open to a breezeless day, I slid onto a stool next to a woman in her early twenties. She didn't introduce herself, but I knew this was Darlene Stone, as she'd sent me her photograph along with the request that I show up already in character. I'd noticed from the photo that hers was a face unburdened by beauty and yet, in person, she exuded a captivating dynamism: a mass of brown curls, upturned nose, and cheeks sprinkled with dark freckles. She wouldn't hold still. Even as I sat down, her nose twitched, no doubt catching a whiff of the body spray I'd doused myself in. Darlene wore what could be either designer or dollar-a-pound: a gray wool poncho and patched wide-legged pants ending in a question mark of yellow combat boots. I wondered if she wasn't warm in this AC-less bar, but she seemed unfazed by the heat. She hadn't specified what she wanted me to wear, but I was glad to see that I'd made the right choice in matching her air of clothing-as-necessity. Clothing was often the hardest choice I had to make when meeting a client—an ill-fitting dress shirt could ruin the illusion of a chaebol's son and an overly clean T-shirt could spoil the impression of a wayward uncle. Indeed, clothes make the invisible man visible: brands give him a position in society and styling gives him soul.

"I ordered you a glass of chardonnay," Darlene said, pushing the base of the wineglass toward me.

This was a test. The character she'd asked me to inhabit was her brother, Serge, a recovering alcoholic who wasn't doing too well on the recovery front (hence the use of overwhelming body spray to mask the whiskey I'd swilled around in my mouth before arriving; like I said, perfectionist). She didn't specify what she wanted out of the interaction, but I assumed it was the usual: practicing how to confront a loved one about the addiction that was deep-frying their liver into funnel cake.

"No thank you," I replied.

She looked at me, her gray-green eyes unnervingly wide-set. Unaccustomed to this level of intense scrutiny (most clients were cowriters in their own fantasies, after all, and few attempted to investigate too closely), I readjusted my glasses, though I didn't break eye contact.

"Too quick," she said.

"What's too quick?"

"Your refusal. It's not believable." She plucked a loose hair that had partially woven itself into the fabric of her poncho. "I mean, where's the split-second hesitation where you negotiate with yourself? There's gotta be that moment of thinking, 'One drink is fine—worse to quit cold turkey and let the thoughts of not drinking subsume you because to focus on not drinking alcohol is to still focus on alcohol and the whole point is to not think about alcohol so might as well have just one drink?' And then, like, maybe you lick your lips as a subconscious sign of thirst—or is that too obvious? Or subvert expectations with a joke like, 'Haha, sis, I'm sober, remember? What are you trying to get me to do? Relapse?' Actually that's a good one, hold on," she said, pulling out her phone and typing

35

away, muttering to herself. "Hesitating and negotiating internally but playing it off on the outside . . ."

After a few seconds I cleared my throat and Darlene snapped her head up, staring at and yet through me with unfocused eyes. The look on her face transported me back ten years to the old Bed-Stuy apartment where my mother hunched over the dining table, working on some sort of manuscript as she had been ever since our abrupt move from Los Angeles to New York. I'd snuck back into the house after one of my romps, and when she'd looked up to see me slinking through the doorway—breaking one of her cardinal rules and bringing the stench of sex back into the apartment—I thought I might get a dressing-down, but instead, she was silent. Her face unreadable as her eyes gazed through me.

I steadied myself with a hand on my knee. "Excuse me," I said, "but maybe you could clarify what exactly you're looking for in this encounter?"

Darlene clicked her phone off and on and off again, her background an unsettling scene from a Hieronymus Bosch painting of a naked woman riding what looked to be a unicorned cat without eyeballs.

"I thought it would be better to just go for it, see what comes naturally, but maybe context is important," she said. "You see, Serge isn't actually my brother. He's a character in my novel, but I'm having such a hard time writing him and the effect he has on Charlene, his sister, and I believe it's because I haven't really experienced what it's like to be the sister of an alcoholic, which is important because apparently pain, especially fictional pain, demands specificity."

"So you're a writer," I said.

"I'm trying." Darlene explained that she was an MFA student in fiction and had been having a helluva time slaving away on a manuscript for the past two years. The characters were lambasted by her classmates as suffering too tragically, or being tragically insufferable. But Darlene was dedicated to tragedy, because wasn't that what great literature was about? What kind of novel would *Madame Bovary* be if the eponymous character simply had accepted life at her station, cheerily raised her child in the countryside, and died of old age surrounded by loved ones? Why read stories at all if living the small tragedies of our own lives suffices? "And that's what art, and life, is about, isn't it?" she said, pouring my glass of wine into her own. "Beauty in the yuck of it all?" She swirled it around, closing one eye and peering at me through the yellow liquid. "So yeah, that's what you're here for—to help me feel pain, specifically."

"That sounds fascinating," I said. "But I'm afraid that's not what I do." Hurting my clients was the exact opposite of my happiness motto. I brushed nonexistent crumbs off my pants and made to stand up. Luckily, the app had measures in place for clients who were not a match. I couldn't afford a second poor review. I pulled out my phone. There was still the better part of an hour before time ran out on the assignment. "I work to make people happy, not unhappy. It's my fault for not fully understanding the assignment today so I will be refunding your fee."

"No, no," she said, hands aflutter. "I'm not being clear! Writers! Good with written words but terrible with speaking, ya know, spoken words. Of course the pain isn't *real* because I'll be playing a character too! I'll be the sister, Charlene! So we're, like, scene partners, yeah? And what you'll *really* be helping me with is understanding my characters, which would be tremendous for my manuscript and, of course, my eventual eternal happiness once this damn thing gets published! Please," she said, "please help. I need to turn something in this semester since I got an extension already and I might not graduate otherwise. You'll be doing me such a solid, seriously!"

Darlene was able to afford my high fee (my fees rose with my renown each year and also with market inflation, but I still allowed for some negotiation—Mari, my oldest client, was grandfathered into a rate that was several times cheaper than what I charged now), and I would be lying if I said this kind of a job, different in its scope, wasn't intriguing. Surprisingly enough, I'd never had a writer as a client before.

"We're both playing parts," she said. "So, all fun, no consequences!"

"Okay," I said, giving in to Darlene's enthusiasm and a bit flattered that she'd chosen me for this creative assignment out of all the other rentals. I was running on autopilot most days, so a challenge would be good for me. I wasn't feeling nearly as mentally depleted at the end of the day as I did in my earlier years, and I missed that emptiness. Craved it.

"It's a bit out of the ordinary," I warned her, "but if it'll help you out, I don't see why not."

"Thank you!" she said, clasping my hands in hers. Her palms were clammy, wet and cold from the condensation of the wineglass. "Seriously, I think this will make a huge difference! Now if you could go back to being Serge . . ."

I lifted her overly full glass and poured a splash back into my own. "Here's to us," I said.

"Wait, but you're—"

I gulped it down before she could finish. "C'mon, sis," I said, indicating that I was back in character. "It's too sad to let you drink alone."

Darlene nodded and reached for her phone again, typing and dictating furiously. "Manipulating familial ties for alcohol . . . action before explanation . . . feeling of guilt . . . inability to stop . . ."

Most people requested an ideal version of the position they wanted filled—be it lover, friend, or child. Even those who hired me to play an ex-boyfriend or ex-coworker to give them a piece of their mind usually desired a happy ending (so often seen on TV and so rarely experienced in real life) so that after the half hour or hour or three hours, I became the best version of their ex-someone, wishing them happiness, or apologizing, or both. All that to say, it had been some time since I'd played a flawed character, and it was difficult not to slide too far into doting brother or overcompensate by being a complete asshole. If Darlene wanted to continue with this assignment—which I now hoped she would so I could provide a more nuanced performance—I would be better prepared after a crash course in alcoholic recidivism with readings of Hemingway or Amis, or I could take real-life courses by lurking on the corner of Canal and Division, watching the lushes sprint through their heady, drunken youth.

"This is gonna be great," said Darlene at the end of our sixty minutes, half of which she spent typing notes on her phone. "I feel like I'm really getting to *know* what dealing with an alcoholic brother is like, which is, yeah, different than I imagined."

I smiled, straightening my back and pushing the third glass of wine aside to indicate that we were back to business mode. "Wonderful," I said. But before I could ask if my services were satisfactory, Darlene continued.

"I didn't really know what to expect because I thought it might be a bit, like, cringe, you know? Or overdone? But it felt pretty natural and I can see how people get into hiring Rental Strangers. I know someone who, she'd never admit it, but she's totally addicted to going on dates with this one guy on the app. Do you think"— she glanced around as though her friend could be hiding in the sun-dappled corners of the bar—"they'll ever get together? I mean, do you think he could actually be into her?"

If it were me her friend was seeing, the answer would be no. I'd had many clients ask me out on a "real" date after our paid dates, but I always reminded them that the person they'd just gone out with was a creation of their own imagination and didn't exist outside of working hours. The more romantic of these clients would insist that they wanted to get to know the *real* me, to which I smiled politely and assured them that they did not.

"Maybe," I said. "We rentals don't really talk to one another."

"Oh," said Darlene. "Why not?"

Did mannequins in a storefront chitchat? No, they simply sold the clothes and the fantasy life they advertised. "I don't know," I said. "I guess we all do our own thing. Better not to get involved in other people's business."

"Just thought I'd ask," said Darlene with a shrug. "In case I need to stock up on tequila and tissues. Anyway, this session was super helpful so, yeah, I'm gonna want to meet pretty regularly. When are you free?"

"Scheduling is on the app," I said. "But the holiday season gets busy, so you'll want to book October and especially November and December dates early."

"Oh, fascinating," said Darlene. "I would love to talk about your work sometime, you know, out of character."

I didn't have a rule against talking about my work on the job, but I preferred not to, for client confidentiality reasons. Though when pressed, I would pretend to give in and vaguely answer a question or two just to make the client feel special.

"Maybe," I said.

"Like, do you sexually fantasize about your clients?"

"What?" I said, unsure I heard right.

"You know, do you ever jerk one out to a hot client after work?"

"No," I said. "Definitely not."

Darlene pursed her lips and scanned my face like she was reading a lengthy text printed from brow to chin. I wondered what she was looking for—would the twitch of a brow or quiver of an iris give away that I was lying? I held my features completely still so as not to betray the truth. It happened rarely, but on some days, the particular shape of a woman's thigh as she sat down, or the curvature of another client's ear, or the pearling of sweat on her temple might feature in my mind's eye as I stared up at the light fixture the next morning. Darlene's face was close enough now that I could connect the dots of the freckles on her nose. I tried to stare through her.

"Boo!" she said, and I flinched as she laughed. "Sorry, you looked like you were frozen and I wanted to make sure you hadn't short-circuited!"

I adjusted my glasses again, feeling irritated at having lost control of my body for a second. It reminded me of the pediatrician's reflex mallet violating my knee, forcing it to spasm and kick like an ass. Even as a child I hated losing control, perhaps because I had so little of it to begin with.

But of all the things I'd mastered over the years, my emotions were top of the list. I tucked the irritation away beneath my tongue and began to wrap up the job, which was already running a few minutes over. "Do you require anything more from me today, or was this satisfactory?"

"No, sir," she said, doffing an invisible hat. "I'm quist satisfiedeth."

I thought, in that moment, that I hated this woman—people like her and Ajay were never satisfied with what life gave them despite having been dealt an objectively winning hand—but I couldn't let this show. The hour was over and I couldn't risk a second one-star review tailing the first. Much to my surprise, Darlene apologized.

"That was mean," she said. "I'm sorry. I know you're just doing your job! I'm the one being weird—like, get it together, Darlene!"

"It's okay," I said.

"You're not mad, are you?"

"No," I said. And I wasn't. What was the point of being mad at a client? Negative feelings were their own kind of attachment, and my first rule was no emotional attachment either way.

"Thank goodness! Okay, well then, I'm gonna go attempt to write and then drink myself to oblivion when it doesn't go well. Till next time!"

I watched her leave, feeling drained in a way that was rare these days, but not unwelcome. I lifted my wineglass, where a mouthful of chardonnay remained, and mimicked the way Darlene had held it up to one eye, squeezing the other shut and viewing the world through a yellow-tinted monocle. Unfortunately, the cloudy condensation cupping the wine meant I couldn't see anything at all.

After sitting for a minute or two, I realized I'd all but forgotten about Ajay's review. The stress of managing Darlene had overtaken my obsession over Ajay's vitriol. I pulled out my phone in a hurry, opening the app and tapping the envelope icon. I thumbed past the requests I'd received in the past few hours to find that yes, the app had agreed to remove Ajay's review. I rolled out a crick in my neck and looked up to smile at someone I thought was the bartender, but then quickly realized was my own reflection in the bar mirror. It was an odd sensation, but one that I'd gotten used to over the years, enjoying it now like a private joke—being a stranger to myself.

CHAPTER 5

The next time I saw Lily, she was stumped while working on a family history report for school. Lily had never met her mother's side of the family since they'd disowned a teenaged Mari as soon as she'd become pregnant with Lily out of wedlock. Lily's real father was somewhere out in the Midwest, unaware that half his genome lived east of the Mississippi. I'd been brought on when Lily was two years old to play father to Lily and husband to Mari— for even though Mari hated her parents' conventional ideas of family, she'd also internalized them. The arrangement was simple: as a long-haul truck driver, I could have a pit stop at home only one night a week. I arrived in time to pick Lily up from school, and left bright and early before she woke up the next morning. It was a ruse that had gone unquestioned for the past eight years, though now that Lily was turning ten, I wasn't sure how long Mari intended to continue.

As for my side of this pretend family, I'd written them out of the equation by placing that branch of the tree on the other side of the world, in Japan.

While wiping down the kitchen counters, I observed Lily from my peripheral vision as she sat cross-legged on her chair, pulled up to the dining table. She wore the same frayed skirt from last week, though this time with a cotton shirt two sizes too big, perhaps Mari's. Lily scratched her head.

"Dad," she said after a few minutes. "What are Grandma and Grandpa's names?"

"Yohsuke and Nana."

"Tanaka?"

"That's right."

"And on Mom's side?"

Mari refused to speak her parents' names, but the branches of Lily's report would be as unbalanced as a single horned stag without them. What would it hurt to make up this side too?

"Ryo and Yumi."

"Also Tanaka?"

"Yes."

Lily scratched her head again. "You and Mom aren't, like, related, are you?"

I snorted and walked over to the dining table, sitting in the chair next to hers. "Tanaka is a common last name."

"Okay," said Lily. And then, after filling in these two branches, she stopped and bit her upper lip, surveying roads and intersections that all led to a single destination: Lily Tanaka. "Dad, when I grow up, will I look like you?"

"What do you mean, Moose?"

"Like, will I look more like you or like Mom?" She paused. "I wanna look like you."

"You'll look like yourself," I said.

She put her pencil down and covered her nose with one hand. "But I don't want that!"

"What's wrong?"

"My nose is too flat, and too round, like Mom's."

I had a client earlier that day with a hooked nose she wore with pride, and in her celebration of it, there was beauty.

"Your nose is perfect."

"No it's not!" said Lily. "Piri says that my nose is like, like, a pancake."

"Who's Piri?"

"A boy in my class."

"Well, I say your nose is perfect, and do you believe some boy in your class or do you believe your dad?"

Lily scanned my face, and I wore my best encouraging look—eyebrows slightly raised, a faint smile, head tilted up signaling honesty and vulnerability.

"I just want to be pretty," said Lily.

"You're something even better," I said. "You're smart."

Lily frowned, her chin dimpled as a peach pit. I realized my mistake too late. Those without beauty desired it and those with beauty are desperate to keep it. In other words, everyone wants to be beautiful.

"You're smart *and* pretty."

"It's okay," said Lily, quiet as resignation. Then, putting a hand on my knee as though I were the one seeking consolation, "You don't have to pretend."

Mari was late coming home again, this time far drunker than she was before. I didn't have an assignment lined up this evening but was still feeling agitated, both because of how I'd said the wrong thing to Lily and because Mari was slipping in her role of wife-eagerly-awaiting-husband's-once-a-week-return, and had been for some time now.

"I'm so sorry," said Mari, her unfocused eyes sliding past me before landing somewhere to the left of where I stood. "It was the, you know . . ."

"New boss?" I said, taking a seat at the kitchen table.

"Yeah," she said as she sank into the chair across the table. "He insisted but it won't"—she slapped the kitchen table—"happen again. What's this?"

Lily's homework, which had been completed hours before, still hadn't been packed away since she'd wanted to show it to her mother, but a strict bedtime had overcome her. She had fallen asleep half an hour before Mari returned home, around the time my phone had buzzed, informing me the assignment was supposedly over.

Mari squinted at the piece of paper, bringing it nearly to her nose. "Ryo? Yumi?"

"I made up your parents' names," I said. "I hope that's okay."

Mari laughed, rocking backward in her chair and nearly tilting over. "Ryo! Yumi! That's great, no, that's great. They would have hated that." Despite her state of inebriation she got up to grab her routine beer from the fridge. "You know they changed their Japanese names to English ones before even leaving Japan? They were both so eager to be someone else, someone better, someone American. And then, when they had me, they wanted to give me an English name too, Mary, but they fucked it up, or maybe I was the fuckup, haha." She opened the can and foam cascaded down her wrist, threatening to stain her blouse cuffs. "Ryo and Yumi. That's great. That's just great." It pained me to see Mari so sloppy—I wanted to snatch the beer from her hands, but I clasped mine together beneath the table instead.

"Oh shit," she said after taking a sip, "I gotta—" She thumped the can down onto the table and ran off to the bathroom, where the sounds of stifled retching reverberated beyond the thin walls. I filled a cup with water and placed it next to her can of beer. Eventually, Mari stumbled out, teary-eyed, jaw clenched.

She slid back into her seat and noticed the glass of water. "Thanks," she said, grimacing at the taste in her mouth. "I made you stay overtime again, huh? When I get my next paycheck I'll give you extra."

"It's really okay," I said, knowing there wasn't any extra to give. I could make time for my oldest repeat client, so long as Mari didn't continue to make a habit of it. "But try to be home on time, for Lily's sake."

At the mention of her daughter, Mari sat up a little taller, which, at five foot three, still wasn't very tall. "Lily's sake?" she said, her mood turning, sudden as a summer storm. "What do you care? I mean, really, who are you to tell me how to raise my daughter?" She reached for the can of beer, tipping its lip toward hers so violently that a trickle of liquid dribbled down her chin. "You think you're better than me?" she said.

No, I wanted to tell her, no I certainly do not. Though Mari thinking I was better was why she'd hired me in the first place. Of course, I didn't remind her of that.

"I'm working myself to the bone to take care of Lily," said Mari. "I don't *want* to go out drinking with my creepy boss. I'm doing it so I can keep my job! So I can feed and clothe her and raise her to do better than me! To be better than, than this." She raised her arms, indicating everything around her, myself included, and then let them flop to her sides. "You wouldn't understand," she said. "I bet your parents paid for your whooooole life, college boy, and now I'm paying for y—"

I put a finger to my lips and motioned over to the bedroom door, where I hoped Lily was still sleeping.

"Do you want to go speak outside?" I said.

"No, no," she said, rubbing her temples and squeezing her eyes shut. She swayed for a minute. "Shit, what was I saying?"

"That you didn't like drinking with your boss," I said.

"Oh," she said, "right, what a creep." And then, scrunching her eyes, "I feel like I was mad about something else, but now I'm not sure what."

"Something that he did," I suggested.

"Oh yeah," she said. "He tried to speak Japanese to me. So gross."

Some people might find my little maneuvers manipulative, but I knew better than to engage in a meaningless argument with a client; tomorrow, when she sobered up, she wouldn't remember and I would act as though it had never happened, which meant that for both of our sakes it would be better if we never got into it at all. Anyway, I had crossed a line bringing Lily into what should have been a business conversation; I could only insist Mari be on time to fulfill our arrangement on the app. Saying that Lily wanted her mom to be home at a certain hour? Well, that was unprofessional. Lily wasn't my client. Mari was. Mari was the one paying and Mari was the one who called the shots. Still, I couldn't forget Lily's slumped shoulders as she glanced at the clock on the microwave, waiting for her mom to return.

"Are you okay?" I asked, as Mari was now looking somewhere between water glass and beer can, her eyes unsure of where to focus.

"I'm fine," she said, a phrase that almost always signaled the exact opposite, but because this was not a personal but professional relationship, I let it go.

"If there's anything I can do, let me know," I said—an equally empty and meaningless phrase.

"I'll be home in time for dinner next week," said Mari, voice subdued. "When I get my next paycheck I'll give you extra."

I wasn't sure if this was her insisting or forgetting that she'd already said this, but it confirmed my suspicion that nothing I said tonight mattered.

"For the record," I said, and only because there would be no record, no recollection, "I do understand. I was also raised by a single mother."

"Huh?" said Mari.

"Nothing," I said, moving Lily's project away from the can of beer. I stood up from the table and walked to the door, pulling on my boots. "You're doing a great job," I said, far too quietly for her to hear. And then, more loudly, "Good night."

Out on the street where the sky remained brushed with the fading pinks of the setting sun, the temperature was finally dropping, and I paused at the landing, watching a couple walk by, hands in each other's back pockets. I'd seen what it was like for a woman to raise a child on her own—and in my mother's case, how lonely and terrible it could be. My father had left when I was so young that I possessed nothing of him but a smudged memory of a white man who would sometimes lift me up onto his shoulders, where I was so high that I could see the pale line of my mother's scalp, which frightened me. To me, my mother was a fortress and her legs were towers I often hid behind, but from that vantage point she looked like a small hill with no defensive advantage, easily vanquished. As I grew older, and taller, I worried about the day I would overtake her, when I would stand straight and see above and past her, but I shouldn't have worried so much. That day never came.

CHAPTER 6

On an overcast Friday morning, I attended a funeral at Green-Wood Cemetery in Brooklyn.

Funerals and weddings were the two staples of my profession. They were similar in a way: the attire, the speeches, the family, and then the hunger and laughter that snuck in like a late guest after the formalities ended. It was at these celebrations of union and departure that I often saw other rentals. We never spoke to one another besides what was necessary for our roles, but it was interesting to see who could pull off a convincing best man speech or who hammed it up too much as a grieving brother. There weren't many of us who stuck it out over the years, though. It was a difficult business that very specific individuals excelled at. If you had any ego, acting was a far better choice; for us, a job well done meant we faded away while only the memory of our role (a funny in-law, a considerate classmate) remained. There was, however, one older man whom I'd seen on the job constantly for the past decade. I didn't even know if he was on the app or if he'd been a practitioner in this field long before there was an app for it since he was probably in his early sixties.

Each time I saw him, he was dressed in a different formal black out-fit (I imagined his apartment was a dark cave lined with polyester and blended wools), with such a generic face that he didn't even need to put on makeup or prosthetics to work his gigs. Observant as I was, it took me months to realize that this man, whose costum-ing was as subtle as wearing different expressions on his face, had attended almost all of the funerals I attended, showing up to work as consistently as the grim reaper himself. At first he would come up to me to make small talk, but after he realized what I was, he didn't bother approaching me again—it wasn't personal, and I understood. It was the other funeral-goers, the people who actually had known the deceased in life, whom we needed to convince—oftentimes con-trary to their own experiences—that the deceased was good, was loved, was talented, was special.

Today, however, the old crow stood next to me, shoulder to shoulder.

"How did you know Brett?" he asked, blowing his nose as family members gave short speeches about their maladjusted son who'd dropped out of high school years ago. Though it was near impossible to hear with the wind and the airplanes overhead, I doubted they'd mention this shameful fact. I nodded along to words I couldn't hear.

"Friend of the family," I said—a classic line, too general to refute and too boring to ask for more details.

"Pity when they die this young, isn't it?" the man said. I could feel his gaze upon me, but I faced forward, unnerved and unsure why he was speaking to me at all.

"Yes," I said, finally turning to face him. Today he wore the air of a professor-of-a-small-college-you-never-heard-of-somewhere-in–New England. "Death is unfair."

"Death is an equalizer; life is unfair."

At that we both fell silent. The fresh wood casket, bright and un-blemished, was lowered into the earth. The family took turns tossing in flowers before cemetery workers laid a tarp over the hole.

"Come and walk with me," said the old man as the crowd dis-persed. It had been a breezy morning, but now the clouds were parting and the sun seemed determined to make up for lost heat. I removed my jacket and tied it around my waist. My character for that day was a grunge musician (a cover, perhaps, for why the de-ceased had dropped out of formal education) and I wore a mustache and ponytailed wig (the wig I wore as Serge, Darlene's "brother," but greased up and tied back). Since I was still on the clock I was deter-mined to stay in character. Also, I must confess, a small part of me wanted to impress this man, who was clearly a master of his craft. Even the handkerchief he took out to mop his brow was frayed just the right amount for a distracted yet distinguished academic. "Do you know who I am?" he asked.

"No," I said.

"Good," he said. "And I don't know who you are, and I do intend on keeping it that way."

The obvious question would be to ask why he was speaking to me at all, then, but I was sticking with the sullen artist role and he, as the didactic professor archetype, would continue without any input from me. We both understood our parts. It was only a matter of playing them out.

"You must be wondering, then, why I decided to speak with you today when I've maintained my distance for quite a long duration. Well, it is no easy matter. As you know, in our line of work, anonymity is tantamount to success, but I've been watching you for some time now. Don't you think observation is key in our profession? But of course, you know that. And I've come to realize that you have been in the field, so to speak, for nearly a decade now, yes, and I suppose I'm approaching you, as in coming nearer through distance, and you are approaching me, as in nearing me through time spent in the craft. For isn't it an art what we do? And so I felt a certain responsibility because I see you have what it takes to really shine in this niche artistic endeavor so I thought to myself, well, old boy, you ought to give this young boy a hand, one freebie. So, there you go."

This time I was at a genuine loss for words. "What?"

"A question, my boy! Don't you have any questions about this calling of yours? An actor 'to ease the anguish of a torturing hour'!"

An English professor with a lust for his old days performing theater, it seemed. Because mother had made me rehearse *A Midsummer Night's Dream* dozens of times with her, I could have given him a ten-word retort: I know of no questions, good sir, adieu, adieu, adieu. But I didn't appreciate the comparison with foolish two-bit actors or the idea that he was poking fun at me, a little hazing of the newbie. Well, I was no newbie.

"I'm good, man," I said.

"Harumph!" said the old man. "I suppose this ends our brief acquaintance. Let no one accuse me of not possessing a generous heart." And, quick as a New York spring, he was gone. Though that very afternoon, at a wake in Long Island City, I saw the old man again, this time looking twenty years older in a loose-fitting suit, trailing the scent of patchouli, his eyes glazed over like the sixties had scrambled his neurons. He didn't glance in my direction even once, and I wondered if maybe I'd missed out on something important. Or perhaps generosity through tutelage was also a role he'd been trying on that morning—and now that he'd taken it off, the impulse was gone. But what could he have illuminated for me? I was a top-rated Rental Stranger; who was he?

CHAPTER 7

Mari was pissed when I saw her again the next week, though this time not at me. I could tell she didn't remember what we'd discussed while she was wasted as she neither apologized nor avoided me. But something must have stuck with her, because tonight she was home in time for dinner, and the three of us sat around the table eating a beef stir-fry I'd prepared for our weekly family meal.

"Can you believe this guy?" she said, spearing beef strips with her fork. Tonight she'd had time to change out of her department store attire and was wearing a faded blue tank top and the stretched-out gym shorts that showed her ample, dimpled thighs. Soon, when the weather turned colder, those shorts would disappear with the warm days until next year. I kept my eyes strictly above the table. "Work hours are already too long!" Mari complained. "I don't care if you're buying the drinks, if you're not paying me overtime, why would I go?"

"Maybe he wants to get to know everyone," I said. "Being new and all."

"Really?" she said, her tone clearly asking, whose side are you on? I couldn't help this way of thinking—turning and turning a situation over in my head and inspecting the different possibilities. On some sleepless nights I wondered if I could've been a lawyer if only I hadn't been so repulsed by the first one I'd met, if only I'd graduated high school, if only I'd been a better son, if only.

"A joke," I said.

"Save your jokes for someone who can afford them."

I glanced at Lily, who was dutifully skewering beef and pepper together to experience a balanced meal in each bite. Drunk Mari had confirmed what I'd been unwilling to acknowledge for a while now—that she and I were getting too comfortable with each other. When we'd started out as pretend husband and wife, we acted as though a more perfect union couldn't exist—a love made sweeter because of my weeklong absences. Back then, Mari called me Prince Charming, a tongue-in-cheek nickname that perhaps hinted at a wish to be saved. And this husband-and-wife act with the devoted but hardworking father entertained Lily when she was two years old and the functioning of her immediate family was all she knew. But as she matured, there was no doubt that the dazzle of our unrehearsed play dimmed as she noticed the worn actors, the dilapidated set, the canned bits. Yet she said nothing. And Mari said nothing. And I said nothing, for it would take a long revision and some new scripted parts to move the play toward a divorced-but-co-parenting narrative, and Mari would be the one paying for the rehearsals.

Lily kept her head down during this spat, willing us to believe she wasn't listening while every pore of her body soaked in the smallest inflections of our tones. Wanting to be a good girl, to keep the peace. An oblivious child would have interrupted; an observant one remained silent. I chewed slowly and kept my gaze on Lily, who was still carefully arranging beef and pepper slices side by side. Mari, who'd stopped calling me Prince Charming years ago, got the hint.

"I'm sorry, sweetie," she said. "All this grown-up talk must be so boring for you. How was school?"

"It was good," said Lily. On our walk back home, Lily had recited the e. e. cummings poem they were memorizing and pointed out isosceles triangles in pitched rooftops of buildings, but now she kept quiet.

"And?" said Mari.

"And what?" said Lily.

"Come on, Moose," I said. "Don't be so obtuse."

At this Lily snorted and finally looked up from her plate. "Obtuse is an angle more than ninety degrees and less than one-eighty, Dad! I'm not an angle."

"You're not an angle, but you *are* my little angel. Also, *obtuse* has a different definition. Do you know it?"

"No, what is it?"

"Why don't you look it up in your dictionary?"

Lily hopped out of her chair and into the bedroom to lift the hefty dictionary off her shelf. Mari watched her leave and placed her fork down on the table, even though she hadn't finished the food on her plate.

"What does it mean?" asked Mari, leaning toward me.

"What does what mean?"

"Obtuse."

"Oh, well, you're about to find out once Lily—"

"Tell me," she said, in a strained whisper, "what it means."

"Slow to understand," I said.

When Lily returned with the dictionary, flipping through the *Ks* and *Ls*, Mari said, "Why don't you ask Mom what *obtuse* means?"

Lily froze, her finger hovering above *obstinate*, and I could almost hear the gears in her head turning. Why hadn't she asked her mother the definition of a word? Likely because she knew, subconsciously, that her mother wouldn't know the answer and didn't want to embarrass her; or was it rather that she was embarrassed by her mother and didn't want to find out, definitively, that her mother did not know what Lily suspected she didn't know?

"Ask me," said Mari.

"Um," said Lily, flipping the pages a little faster. "'Obtuse, adjective, lacking a sharpness or quickness of intellect. Insensitive.'"

"Like me," said Mari, with a harsh laugh.

Lily buried her face a little deeper into the thick book.

I sat between mother and daughter, unsure of what to say next. The last time Mari had been this prickly was when she'd sprained her ankle and couldn't go to work for a few weeks, but at that time Lily was six and a half and hadn't noticed the way her mother snapped at her father—the pretense of love obliterated by pain—or the fact that her father didn't take time off to help his struggling wife. Believability was difficult with this long-term assignment, and made even harder by the fact that I had no blueprint of a father. My only guidance was of the fathers on the page and screen. In those cases, they were the cause of conflict, not the mediators.

The silence at the table turned heavy, threatening import, and I had to try and guide the mood back to what I imagined as a happy family dinner. "What's the next word in the dictionary?" I said at the same time as Mari pushed herself back from the table, stating, "I'm full." I stood up to help her pack her leftovers for lunch, but she waved me off and said, "No, you go help Lily learn. That's your job."

Perhaps this was the cause of her bitterness. Her job—the one that she'd been slaving away at for years, that still gave her nothing but a measly paycheck in return—was taking away time she could have spent with her daughter. My job, on the other hand, was exactly this—to help raise her child in her stead, what she believed she couldn't do well enough because she wasn't smart enough, well-educated enough. And she had to believe that I could do for Lily what she couldn't. But from time to time, when life pressed down on her, squeezing her for more than she had to give, she couldn't help but grind down to rinds wondering if I was worth the juice.

When I first met Mari nearly eight years ago at a prearranged spot near the Columbia campus, where the coffee tasted of tin and the pastries of heaven, she'd arrived in an oversized, secondhand coat. She'd been running, a high blush seared across pale cheeks. Back then there wasn't even a trace of gray in her temples. "Sorry I'm late," she said. "I had to drop off my daughter at day care." And then, after a quick once-over, "You're younger than I expected."

Mari's email had been riddled with grammatical errors, and I could tell that she was unable to relax into the hard-backed chair pressed tightly against the one behind her, for at her right elbow was a hunched man reading Borges and at her left was another one reading Baudelaire, and behind, a woman with unkempt hair who was likely an astrophysicist or a musical genius. Mari was clearly unaccustomed to being surrounded by those who toiled in mind not body, and yet she had been the one to choose this meeting spot. Why? Because despite her own discomfort in these spaces, this was what she idealized. This was what she wanted for her rental partner to represent: someone she felt she could not find on her own and could only pay to possess—an intelligent man in a salt-of-the-earth way. Even though she had full creative control over my profession, she still could not imagine anyone besides a blue-collar worker as her life partner. Even her fantasies hit a glass ceiling. And so I came into being: a truck driver who listened to NPR on the road and read German philosophers at rest stops. Once she confirmed that I held myself with ease in places like this, it was a done deal.

The way Mari saw it, I would be Lily's sherpa, leading her to pinnacles of intellect and privilege that Mari could never navigate. Above all, what Mari wanted for her daughter was a better, easier life where numbers could be calculations for a company's quarterly earnings and not one's own precarious balancing of payments for food versus shelter. And for that, Mari was willing to sacrifice— there would be no strange men in the house just because Mari was feeling lonely some nights. And Lily would never have to waste time wondering who her "real" father was. Instead, she would grow up with a complete family—husband, wife, kid. Even though I would show up only every Thursday, rain or shine, the rest of the time Lily would know I was out there, on the road, drumming my fingers on the wheel and thinking about my little girl. She could rest assured knowing I loved her and that I would return. After being kicked out of her own home and abandoned by the man who'd knocked her up, Mari knew not to trust the weak bonds of love and family—so what she created was the bond of a legal contract, signed not with feeling but with cash.

As Lily and I read over *obumbrant* and *obvallate*, I kept an eye on Mari's back while she scrubbed the dishes. I was delivering on my side of the contract as always, and yet I had enough experience to recognize how when my clients found out they'd gotten exactly what they thought they wanted, they were often disappointed by their own lack of imagination. Mari, to her credit, had held on to her belief in this idealized future for her and her daughter for a long time—but the wear was starting to show. Now that Lily had begun noticing her mother's intellectual limits, I wondered how much more of a bruising Mari's ego could take. Lily was too kind to point out that she, at nine, was already outstripping her mother's vocabulary, but this only heightened Mari's shame. I had to help Mari remember that her goal for Lily was still worth pursuing: that the dead-end job, and the long hours, and the creepy bosses would be worth it for that email in the spring of Lily's senior year that read *Dear Ms. Tanaka, We are delighted to inform you that the Committee on Admissions and Financial Aid has voted to offer you a place in . . .* , and that Lily's advancement didn't mean Mari would get left behind. As Lily sounded out *obviation*, I wondered if I was thinking too far ahead. We'd never discussed how long Mari intended this job to continue, and I had no idea if she'd want me around as a governess-adjacent until Lily left the nest. At the beginning, I'd wondered how long I would have to pretend to be a little girl's father, and after a few years I'd taken it for granted that I would be a teenager's dad.

"What's wrong?" said Lily.

"Nothing, a dizzy spell," I said, releasing the table's edge I hadn't realized I was gripping. "Time for you to get ready for bed."

While tying my boot laces before I left the apartment for the evening, I looked up and gave Mari my most winsome smile. "You're doing great," I said, now at eye level with her legs—those legs which had carried her across state lines as a teenager, which now walked department store floors during long working hours of selling high-waisted leggings to the athleisure class, and which bore beautiful dimples and resilient stretch marks. "You're a good mother."

Mari bit her lip, but wouldn't look me in the eyes. "Good night," she said.

I could taste astringent pepper on my tongue as I walked out of the building. I'd been distracted while sautéing and the meal tee-tered on the verge of charring. I wanted to run back upstairs and apologize to Mari, and let her know that this dish didn't represent my best efforts and that I could try harder, that I was worth keeping around.

Of course, I did nothing but make my way down the street, look-ing up at darkening blues blanketing the fading light, and then back down at a street vendor packing up his produce for the evening. The city was quiet, and I opened up the app to review my upcoming clients, distracting myself from any further thoughts of Lily, Mari, and a future I had no control over.

CHAPTER 8

The second time I met up with Darlene, I arrived drunk. Fake drunk. We were meeting at a café in the East Village where the seats spilled out onto the sidewalk and butted up against square tree plots fertilized by cheap beer and dogs who couldn't read the signs about curbage.

"Sup," I said, slowing down my blinks and unfocusing my vision. I sipped a beer that I had stowed in a coffee mug. Dribbled a little down my chin the way Mari had. Wiped at it with a sleeve. Smirked.

Darlene had already taken a seat outside beneath a golden-boughed gingko and she was immersed in a novel, scratching her head with a pen. She wore overalls, one of the straps undone with the bib flapping open, revealing a plain white T and a flat chest.

She had informed me over the app messenger that she would already be in character as Charlene. Darlene as Charlene underlined a sentence in the novel with her pen. "Have you been drinking?"

"What, no. Of course not."

"It's not even noon."

"What're you reading?" I asked, my consonants floating one over another like alphabet soup.

"Murakami," she said. "It's my guilty pleasure. Once you've read one, you've read them all, but that doesn't mean I won't have another slice of cake."

Murakami had been one of my guilty pleasures too, as a child, for his books were filled with explicit sex scenes. Though what I remembered now was not the ways in which sex happened (and it did seem to just happen, without preamble), but rather a scene about skinning a man alive. That this was the scene I read and reread at age seventeen—at the cusp of my troubles with my mother—should have warned me about the darkness occupying my mind and the anger worming its way out.

"How's business school?" I said.

"It's okay," she said. "Lotta work."

"Mmmhm," I said. "And?"

"And . . . the administrators are so lazy! I mean, how hard is it to change the date on an email you send out every year and how long does it take to get a student onto a list-serv that they should be on anyway and why do class lists come out like the week before classes start and . . ." The complaints went on: a lengthy rant about everything from AC-less rooms to some guy in her "learning team" who underlined every other sentence of her peer-reviewed assignments and commented "?????" Finally, after a solid fifteen minutes, she took a breath.

"Wow," she said. "That felt great."

I raised a brow. "For Charlene or Darlene?"

"Both, I guess," she said. "Does this work feel like therapy for you too?"

Certainly not in the traditional sense, as I aimed to fully inhabit my roles, but if therapy were expansive enough to encompass purpose, then my work was therapy in that it gave me a reason to live—a way to redeem myself from the wrongs of my past.

"You mean do I feel like a therapist?" I said, deflecting that question with another, though the answer to which was, oftentimes, yes. "No," I said. "I try to stay true to each character, so unless the character is a therapist . . ."

"You can be anyone?" said Darlene. "Like a therapist or a urologist or a playwright?"

"Sure," I said. "Or a marine biologist or a CEO or a vampire."

"Where'd you learn that?" said Darlene.

"My mother," I answered without thinking. And then, noting Darlene's cocked eyebrow, added, "Actress."

"Someone I've heard of?" asked Darlene.

"No," I said, the slug of warm beer making me sweat in the late-September heat. "Definitely not. Anyway, back to Charlene?"

Darlene shifted, and the immediate subtle slump in her bearing from straight back to slightly hunched surprised me. The way she could change her demeanor to embody someone else's in an instant reminded me of the old man I ran into from time to time.

"I'm tired," she said, cupping a cheek in her hand. "Everyone in the world tires me out."

"Sounds like you don't have many friends," I said, wiping my glasses with the hem of my shirt.

"Friends are wack," she replied, twirling her pen between middle and ring fingers. "You know what I mean. You don't have friends either." The sentiment was clearly intended for Serge, the reckless alcoholic who'd borrowed up all the money and goodwill from the people around him. But through her direct eye contact, I felt her poking around, trying to finger the edge of the Serge mask to peek underneath, telling me she knew that I too was alone. Perhaps more alone than Serge.

It wasn't like I never had friends. Back in LA, I'd make friends at school easily, but then lose them when Mother and I moved from one school district to the next. I remember them now as though they had stayed eight or twelve or fifteen forever, a Guess Who? board of floppy hair, acne, and long-sleeved shirts sporting skater brand logos. After moving to New York, when I was filled with rage and always doing the opposite of what my mother told me, I skipped out on school and fostered friendships of a different kind—the bartender who pretended I wasn't underage, the librarian too grateful for company to care that I should've been in school, and the food cart guy who handed me free sodas with my shawarma. Those days roaming the streets taught me that friendship is transactional and that most adults in this city of eight million are lonely. And now—I'd found a way for those types of reciprocal relationships to pay the rent.

I looked away from her first, tugging the mask back down. "Who needs friends," I said. "When we have each other."

"I don't know," said Darlene, breaking character by straightening up again.

"Don't know what?"

"I don't know if he'd be straightforward like that. I mean, it's a bit Disney, isn't it? Of course he might believe it, and of course he wants to do right by her, but he's . . ." She pressed her pen to her forehead so hard that an indent from the clip's top lingered. "He's too scared to say it out loud."

"Okay."

"And weak. Selfish, even."

"Most people are."

"And maybe doesn't think he's good enough for her. Not just for her, but for his family. For anyone."

"Sure."

"I just don't think he'd believe in himself enough to even offer to be dependable. To be there for her. He would tell her, 'You should make more friends' when what he means is, 'I can be your only friend.' He cuts when he means to calm. Wait, that's a good one, let me write that down."

I watched as she uncapped her pen and pulled out her phone, as though ready to scribble on its black glass surface, and then, realizing her mistake, looked from hand to hand like she couldn't make the technological leap from analog to digital. I couldn't help but laugh.

"Yeah, that's good!" said Darlene. "Serge would totally laugh at someone else's foibles."

The laugh hadn't come from Serge, but from me. I'd felt mean in that moment, unaccustomed to being told that I wasn't doing my job right, so I'd wanted to see if I could knock Darlene's confidence off-balance, as though it were a stack of blocks. Maybe I still had some ego left in me after all.

"That's the type of hurt he's so good at," she continued. "The unintentional kind. The kind where you want to be nice and good but when you're face-to-face with someone you're meant to love, you can't even lift your arms, much less hold them close, and you wonder if maybe you're not even trying that hard, or if there's just something defective in you that you're not capable of kindness. A deep-rooted selfishness that only serves to hurt those around you. Though," she said, clicking the lid of her pen back on, "maybe that's asking too much."

I took another long sip of beer. The problem with the role as

Darlene described was not that it was too hard but that it was too easy. It was as simple as reaching back into my past and channeling my teenage self, blind to the pain of my mother. And yet I wasn't sure if I could do it or if I should do it, because, if I was being honest with myself, one of the main reasons I worked as a Rental Stranger (besides earning the money necessary to live) was to repent—rebalance the cosmic scales by making happy in equal measure to where I'd made hurt. I wasn't sure if I could ever fully atone for what I'd done, but I was trying. What would it mean, then, for me to help someone by regressing? Would it undo the hard work I'd put into running away from the teenager I'd once been? Draping an arm behind the back of my chair, I looked past Darlene at the gingko leaves down the street, always the first to turn color, heralding the start of cooler days ahead.

"Let's go get a drink," I said.

"You know you're not supposed to."

"Don't be a hard-ass, sis."

"Fine," said Darlene. "There's a bar across the street that has an all-day happy hour. But don't tell Mom."

Three drinks in, I tilted my head up toward the dark wood paneling of the bar, the international flags strung across its ceiling seeming strangely obscene with the flaps waving in a weak AC breeze, Jamaica tickling China while Switzerland looked on. I hadn't eaten anything for lunch, and the drinks were hitting me faster than I'd expected.

"What're you afraid of?" asked Darlene, looking a little cross-eyed herself.

"I dunno," I said, wiping at a sticky patch of the wooden table with a waxy napkin. "Disappointing people, I guess." Was that right? That seemed right.

"That's lame," said Darlene. "You should live for yourself."

"You're really telling me that?" I said. "I'm the one drinking all day every day."

Darlene laughed. "Oh yeah, I forgot. I think I'm drunk."

"Me too," I said. We both laughed at that.

"This is fun," said Darlene, and I was surprised to find that she was right. I was having fun, genuinely. Darlene clipped and unclipped the strap of her overall. She continued, "I honestly don't think I've had this much fun in a while. It feels like I'm still working on my novel but, like, there's not as much pressure. It's great. My parents hate that I'm doing this whole writing thing, but even more than that, they'd hate if I tried it and didn't do well. Like, they think it's easy. And it would be embarrassing if I failed. As if my failings were their failings, and, like, in a way I am made up of them, so maybe if I suck then it is their fault, haha. Actually"—she shifted a bit in her chair—"what do your folks think of your job?" said Darlene. "Your mom being an actress and all."

What would my mother think? I tried to conjure an image of her, but all I could see was her headshot—a pale face with dark bangs, a single beauty mark on her upper left cheek like punctuation announcing her visage complete. The light in her eyes shone like she was in on the private joke of life, but her mirthless lips betrayed the bitter punchline. "We don't really talk," I said.

"Oh, I'm sorry," said Darlene, and I hated her look of sympathy more than anything else. This was why I never told anyone about my life—I was whole, self-contained as a balloon, so why did other people always approach with sharpened nails?

"It's fine, really," I said. "And much better than being constantly judged."

"Sure," said Darlene, like she didn't really believe it. And maybe it was the alcohol, or maybe the balloon was leaking, because in that moment I wasn't sure I believed it either. And then she continued, "Well, I think what you're doing is super interesting. You're super interesting. My life, on the other hand, is nothing but writing. All the normal people I know left in the great West-to-Tech migration, so the only ones left in the city are pretentious assholes. Don't worry," she said, "I'm aware I'm one of them." She fished the cherry out of the dregs of her old-fashioned and popped the candied fruit into one cheek. "It's nice," she said, "to talk to someone who isn't in the arts. We're parasites, you know? We pretend like we know so much about life and love and the eternal, but we don't do anything except discuss life and love and the eternal over critter wine. You, on the other hand—you must've really lived a life. You've experienced what we merely scribble down. You're walking art."

I wondered if this was Darlene's way of comforting me as I slid down into my seat, allowing myself to feel comforted, to breathe. "It's really not as exciting as all that," I said. "Anyone can do what I do."

"Including me?" said Darlene.

"Depends," I said. "You have to commit to your part."

"Duly noted, dearest brother of mine," she said, motioning for the check as both of our phones vibrated, signaling the end of our time together. "I shan't slack no more."

CHAPTER 9

Later that evening, after sobering up a bit and thoroughly rinsing with mouthwash, I was introduced to Yena, a six-year-old girl whose mother, Shiyeon, had hired me as a boyfriend to introduce the idea of Mommy finding a new daddy to her little girl.

"This is Mommy's friend Jung," said Shiyeon, tucking her bobbed black hair behind her ears. Despite the temperature outside, their brownstone was kept cool, nearly cold, and little Yena, who wore a teal-blue cardigan buttoned neatly over a cream lace midi dress, shivered as she said hello to me, with a slight bow of her head. I wondered if she always dressed this way, like she could hop up on a piano bench, play a Chopin étude, and hop back down to curtsy. I noted the Steinway in the living room.

Shiyeon wore the adult version of Yena's outfit: a sky-blue silk jacket with pearl buttons covering an elegant cream dress underneath. The three of us stood in the foyer, me pretending to admire the Matisse above the shoe rack while Yena shifted her weight from foot to foot like she wanted to dash away but her well-honed manners kept her standing there, looking at my socked feet.

"Let's eat," said Shiyeon, motioning to the dining room, where surprisingly small individual portions of rice, mackerel, and banchan already lay on a large oak table.

"How old are you?" I asked Yena as I took a seat in one of the high-backed wooden chairs.

"Six," she said into her table setting.

"Yena, look people in the eye when you're speaking to them," said Shiyeon.

"Six," said Yena, looking me in the eyes, and then quickly looking away to grab her bowl of rice.

"And don't lift your bowl like that," said Shiyeon. "You're not a beggar."

I smiled at Yena with what I hoped was a touch of sympathy as she sat rigid in her slightly boosted seat, arms at 90-degree angles.

I steered clear of dishes with an abundance of gochugaru or sesame seeds in them, as I didn't want to know what Shiyeon would think of a slob who'd unwittingly flash red flakes and pale kernels stuck between his teeth.

After dinner, Yena played a piece on the Steinway (though it was a Beethoven sonata and not Chopin) and when she curtsied I clapped enthusiastically. "You're very talented!" I said. Yena covered her face and ran to her mother's side, whispering in her ear.

"She likes you," said Shiyeon later, while showing me to the door. "She thinks you're handsome."

"She's sweet," I said.

"She's lazy," said Shiyeon, "but that's fixable. And now I know," she said, the shine of a pearl button on her jacket catching the light as she turned toward me, "that if I bring a man home he'll have to be as good-looking as you."

"Shouldn't be too difficult," I said.

Shiyeon laughed without showing her teeth. "Yena is too much like her father, but it is a relief that she at least takes after me in her good tastes," she said, her eyes sweeping me from head to toe. "Maybe you could come back. We often head to our house upstate on weekends, but we are available Wednesday and Thursday afternoons. Perhaps a constant male presence in Yena's life would be good for her, at least until I circle around to finding a new partner."

My schedule was filling up, which meant Wednesday afternoons were mostly booked by various clients. The only constant on my calendar was Thursday afternoons and evenings dedicated to Lily. Shiyeon would pay multiples above what Mari did, and I could use the money. My dream was that one day I'd buy out the owner of my little apartment and could call this dressing room for my citywide one-man-show my permanent home. I'd lived in rentals my whole life, and though this never bothered me as a child (what does a child know besides his sphere, small as where his legs can take him?), I remembered the way my mother would glance at for-sale ads for houses in Realtor office windows, and over time I came to understand that we were second-class citizens, subjecting ourselves to the sounds of our neighbors, to dilapidated appliances uncared for by those who came before and those who would come after, to carpets dusted with the epidermis of strangers. Though my savings were not enviable, that I was able to save money at all was a testament to my abilities as a hard worker, a quality my mother had always espoused. To her, hard work and the American dream were two hands clasped together in prayer to Uncle Sam in the sky, who'd rain down dollars like manna from heaven to those who toiled. And I toiled. I could have toiled to become the star of a more lucrative field—"real" acting, Hollywood—but that was what my mother had chased, and as it turned out, what did you need to make it in Hollywood? Money!

I took one last good look around the brownstone. I could see myself spending Thursday afternoons here, in this single-family unit with central air-conditioning instead of a box fan propped in the window, and where undoubtedly a maid did all the cleaning so that I wouldn't have to.

"I'm sorry," I said. "I have prior commitments, but if you find any open spots on my calendar, you are more than welcome to book me for those times."

Shiyeon's face betrayed no emotion, but the way she folded her hands in front closed off her stance. I could tell she wasn't a woman to go out of her way for anyone.

"Have a good evening," she said, opening the door for me.

I nodded my head and left, down the stairs, out the gate. Lost in the thought that Lily would look good in teal blue, I nearly stepped on a rat as it scurried past. No matter the riches, the city is still the city: out here everyone treads the same vermin-infested streets.

CHAPTER 10

Rosh Hashanah was a school holiday, so Lily and I took a trip to visit Grand Central. Despite having grown up in New York City, she and her mother rarely traversed south of 150th. This time, it was me who held on tightly to Lily's hand to not lose her in the crush of suits and briefcases.

She wore her nicest outfit, a pastel-pink romper with ties at the shoulders; the two other times she'd worn it were the first day of school and her ninth birthday. It was already beginning to run small, the hem of the pants creeping up her shin. Since it had been bought secondhand, the shoulder ties were looser for the wear, and every so often I bent over to readjust or retie the bows.

Walking through the station, we admired the constellations ("A map!" exclaimed Lily) overhead in the aquamarine sky that told time in the old way, and the golden clock in the center of the hall, which told time in the new. A mother urged her two teenaged boys to stand together for a photo as they jostled each other and pulled faces. It was so predictable, these parts that the family members played (father off to the side and busy with his phone—work, perhaps). I wondered if they knew it too, deep down, that they were acting according to a script.

Lily squeezed my fingers. She hadn't done it intentionally, but I could see that she was watching this family with unironic interest, and her hands communicated what her words would not.

"Let's send a photo of you to Mom," I said.

"Okay!" she said, lighting up at the idea. "Or maybe we can take one together?"

I preferred not to be photographed, but Lily looked so excited by the possibility of a half-family portrait that I couldn't refuse. I tapped the father of the family I'd been watching on the shoulder, seeing that he was not replying to work emails but rather looking up common English phrases and practicing them under his breath. As I mimed a camera shutter and asked if he could take a photo for us, I wondered how much longer this button-pressing motion would signal picture taking; my younger clients mimed phone calls not with the thumb and pinkie but with a flat palm.

"That sounds great!" said the man, hitching his backpack farther up his back and sliding his own phone into his breast pocket.

Lily and I posed in front of the clock while the man proved himself his wife's equal in enthusiastic photography, shooting from every angle and elevation, urging us to "close!" and "happily, happily!" When I thought he was done, he shook his head and indicated that Lily, though she was far too old for it, should sit on my shoulders.

I was going to thank him and take my phone back when Lily said, quietly, "It's okay, I'm too heavy." So I had no choice but to hoist her up onto my shoulders.

"Wow," said Lily, giggling. "Everyone looks so small from up here! Like ants!"

This, of course, was an exaggeration—but I smiled, and the man exclaimed in a language I'd never heard before, rushing to show me the photo. I unlocked the phone at his gesturing and Lily slouched over the crown of my head to see.

"It's great," I said, and I was surprised that it actually was. Lily beaming, pointing outwards, and me, solidly beneath her, eyes crinkled in a genuine smile. We looked connected as though sculpted out of the same marble, a statue made to last.

A message popped up on my phone from the app. It was Darlene, and the preview read, *Dearest brother, doth thou hast free time on* . . . Still holding on to Lily's leg with one hand, I fumbled a bit before clicking the screen off.

"Who was that?" said Lily, teetering forward to read my phone.

"It's probably spam," I said. The Rental Stranger app allowed you to change its name and logo on your home screen. I had mine set to RS Messenger with a speech bubble icon.

"But she called you brother."

"These things can get very sophisticated."

"It didn't look like spam."

"Like I said . . ."

"Dad," she said, her voice strained as her hands gripped my hair, "are you lying?"

The man who'd taken the photo couldn't understand what Lily was saying, but having two children of his own had given him a sixth sense of when privacy was needed. He ducked out with a "see you later" back to his wife, who was still trying to corral the teens into a normal photo.

I couldn't see Lily's face, but I could feel her chest beginning to rise and fall quickly against the back of my head as though she were about to cry. Mari told me that even as a baby, Lily rarely cried—instead, she patted her mother's back as Mari held her, walking around the too-small apartment, crying in frustration at her own ineptitude with no one in the world to console her but her own child. Even as a baby, Lily seemed to understand that in the Tanaka household, they could only afford enough tears for one. So the quaver in Lily's voice was alarming as she repeated her question. "Do I have . . . an aunt?"

I lowered Lily to the ground as she wiped at her nose.

"Moose—" I took a step forward and Lily retreated a step back.

"Tell me the truth!" said Lily. Her voice, like her mother's, was naturally loud, and a goldendoodle on a leash stopped to sniff in our direction. I gave the dog's owner a look that I hoped read as father-doing-his-best-to-deal-with-his-child's-tantrum.

Turning back to Lily, who now had her arms crossed, I replied, "It's complicated."

"But she's not on the family tree."

"She's—unwell."

"Is that why we don't see her?"

"Precisely."

"Oh."

Lily did not hold my hand again as she walked through the mid-afternoon crowd and I followed closely behind. Eventually, she wandered into a novelty store filled with New York taxicab-themed stationery and toys. The cashier hi-sweetied Lily, who smiled politely back and then browsed the cards printed with pandas and stickers of yellow taxicabs (their own endangered species) before turning to me with a frown. "Dad," she said gravely, "lying is bad."

I would have laughed if I wasn't so wound up, worried about this aunt who had appeared like an unwelcome guest to our party of three with Mari. If lying was bad, then I was evil reincarnate because, like the cosmological turtles, my lies went all the way down.

"You're right," I said. "But, you know, sweetie, lying isn't always bad." I thought I heard the salesclerk clear her throat so I shepherded Lily back out onto the concourse, away from nosy employees trying to co-parent through their judgment. "For example," I continued, "a lie by omission—that means leaving something out—can make someone happy. Let's say your friend got a really bad haircut. Maybe it's better not to tell them at all, or when they ask how it looks, to say, 'It looks good.' Sure it's a lie, but their hair is going to grow out anyway, right? Because if you point out that the haircut is terrible, you'll make them self-conscious and miserable. And what's the use in that? So maybe if the ends justify the means, and you tell a lie to make someone happy, lying isn't all bad."

"So if a lie makes someone happy, then it's good to lie?"

"Sometimes," I said. "Sure."

Lily's furrowed brow reminded me of Mari when she didn't fully understand a word I'd just said—but in this instance I was the inscrutable word.

"So does that mean, like, you lie to me to make me happy?"

"No," I said. "Of course not."

"I want to meet my aunt," said Lily.

"You can't."

"Why not?"

"She's not well."

"I'll visit her at the hospital! When Piri broke his arm, our class went to see him in the hospital and then everyone signed his cast. And, like, Janet told me that Nathan told her that Piri was happy I came."

"That you came, specifically?"

"I mean, that we all came," said Lily, biting her lip.

"And then what happened? Did Piri get better?" I said, sensing a potential diversion.

"Yeah," said Lily. "But he wasn't as good at dodgeball after, and he used to be the best, so he was kinda mad." Lily gripped my fingers again as we walked through the specialty foods market, and she continued on about Piri's forays into soccer, his funniest jokes to date, and his love of video games. From time to time she would catch herself and try to mention another classmate, but somehow those tributaries always fed into the central river of her crush. Though it was troubling to see Lily becoming more like my adult clients who were obsessed with love, I was relieved that the intruding aunt was all but forgotten.

And if only she'd been truly forgotten, maybe things would have turned out differently.

*

On my way home on the 2 train, I considered sending the photo to Mari, but couldn't compose an appropriate message. Would seeing this remind her of the bond that Lily and I had formed and thereby solidify the need for my job to continue? Or would it bother her that the two of us looked like a solid unit without her? Or maybe she would think this photo was overstepping some unspoken rule and that by sending it to her I was announcing my permanent presence in their lives. Would she hate that? Like it? Or maybe she would pull the photo up from time to time, not only to look at Lily, but to see my face and feel glad that she'd chosen me all those years ago.

I shut my eyes. This line of thinking was troublesome—indicative of the type of attachment that would break my first and most important rule.

I opened my camera roll and deleted all forty-four photos that the man had taken, my picture count returning to a familiar zero.

CHAPTER 11

In Union Square, at the south side's low steps, a circle of white men dressed as swamis drummed and danced in sweat-soaked fervor. I wasn't sure if they were selling religion, CDs, or entertainment—regardless, I wasn't buying.

I moved to sit on the steps facing the chess tables, where players layered up in two hoodies (it was breezy, but only one or at most one and a half hoodies seemed necessary) sat at plastic folding tables, boards prepped and ready, an empty seat across from them set to lure opponents with overinflated egos and five dollars to burn.

I brushed my long, black hair out of my face and squinted out over the midday crowd. I'd arrived twenty minutes early and wasn't sure why. Maybe it was because Serge felt like a character I needed time to sink into, or maybe the strange affinity I felt toward him meant I wanted to spend a little more time in his skin. Despite my initial worries, it was refreshing to be paid to be a cynical character for once—the selfish, self-destructive yet charismatic guy who was "wasting his potential," as though potential were as quantifiable as hours in a day or dollars in the wallet.

What would Serge think as he sat here, watching all these ass-holes rushing from one place to the next, like arriving to their desti-nations on time made any difference in the world? The only person Serge had to worry about was himself, and he wasn't even doing a great job of that. And he didn't care. I leaned back onto my elbows.

I'd had a bit of a scare the past weekend at a party in K-town, where the birthday girl, after five shots in quick succession, rubbed up next to me on the couch of the private karaoke room.

"You're Grace's date?" she'd said, nuzzling into my shoulder.

Grace had gone to the bathroom, but I noticed others glancing our way—transcribing the scene into gossip.

"That's right," I said, keeping my hands on my lap.

"Do you like her? You can tell me, I'm her best friend."

"She's great," I said. "Do you need anything?" I asked as I made to get up.

"No, wait," she said, tugging me down by the pant leg. "But, like, how did you meet? She's sooo bad with men."

"Hinge," I said.

"Show me your profile," she said.

"I deleted it," I said.

"Really?" said the birthday girl, cocking her head to one side. "But, like, you've only been on two dates. Are you that serious about her?"

I glanced toward the door, but Grace was nowhere in sight. Everyone else was loudly blessing the rains down in Africa and I wasn't sure what this girl was trying to get at. Did she want to see if I was good enough for her friend, or steal me away?

"I only date one person at a time," I said.

"That's funny," said the girl, her hand now definitely on my upper thigh. She squeezed. "Oh my gosh," she said. "You're not one of those, like, rental people, are you? Grace would totally do that, she's so desperate."

I smiled, taking her hand in mine for a brief moment. "If I were a rental, would you rent me?"

The birthday girl glanced down, suddenly shy, and smiled.

"Well, I'm not one," I said, returning her hand to her own lap. "And I don't want your best friend to get the wrong idea."

It was rare for someone to ask me straight up if I was a rental, but from time to time I could tell by the disbelief in some people's faces that they were suspicious of what I was selling. Those were trying assignments—ones where a family member or so-called friend was always trying to catch me out. To those folks with their pinhole sphincters I wanted to say, relax and enjoy the show—we're putting it on for you, after all.

"You're here early." Darlene had snuck up from the side, interrupting my thoughts. She sat on the step next to me without bothering to brush off what looked like dried pigeon droppings.

I tried to settle back into Serge's nonchalance, waving away intrusive thoughts of a near bad review. ("She's always like that," Grace had reassured me after I'd given her a brief rundown of the incident. "*She's* the one who can't keep a man.")

"Nothing much else to do," I said.

"Really? No other clients? I thought October was busy?"

"I meant that as Serge," I said.

"Oh, my apologies, dearest brother."

I sat up, readjusting my glasses. "About that. Please don't refer to me as your brother over the app messaging system."

"Oh, why not?"

"A client of mine saw your message, which caused"—I gestured with a hand—"complications."

"Well, don't your clients know you're being rented out by other people?"

"Not a client exactly, but a client adjacent."

"What the hell does that mean?"

"Like a client's . . . ward."

"And prithee tell what doth thou meanst by such convolutions?"

"A kid, okay! Someone who thinks I'm her dad."

Darlene had a way of provoking me, but it was my fault for giving in. I immediately regretted my outburst—even though I did, secretly, enjoy her startled silence. She blinked in rapid succession.

"Anyway," I said, eager to move on, "there is a scheduling system for arranging meeting times. The messenger isn't to chat; it's more for last-minute logistics. It's my fault for indulging in scheduling with you over the messenger, but from now on please use the scheduling system for future meetings."

I could tell Darlene wanted to ask more about the child who thought I was her father, but to her credit, she tamped down her curiosity. "Wanna walk around a bit?" she said instead.

"Sure," I said, shaking out the stiffness in my legs and twisting my lower back, which had been pressed against the edge of a concrete step.

We ambled into the park, passing three high schoolers playing hooky and smoking weed by the flagpole, their laughter ringing out as the flag snapped in the wind and geese flew south in checkmark formation.

"Then how do I text you?" said Darlene.

"What do you mean?"

"Like, what if Charlene wants to text Serge? It's one of the main ways they communicate with each other since he's kinda hard to get a hold of." Darlene was ramping up again, which made me relax. "I

84

was considering setting the novel in the 1980s to avoid texting and all that, but eighties people really love gatekeeping the eighties. One of my professors was all, 'That's *not* how we talked in the eighties.' Whatever! Did you talk to every person in the eighties? It's totally possible that someone in the eighties said 'Bad Bitch.' Anyway, why don't you give me your number?"

I'd given out my number before for short-term assignments, for example, during a social function when a client wanted me to text them continually over the course of an hour so that they would appear popular, but those were contained engagements and I could delete the contact swiftly after. This, however, seemed murkier. I may have found a little solace in Serge's attitude toward life, but I couldn't carry him with me all day every day. It would be a hard switch of gears from Serge to Jeremy the animal shelter volunteer, or Serge to Daryl the CEO's son, or Serge to Lily's father.

"We can text over the app as brother and sister, but you'll have to book texting time."

"Geez," she said, blowing a strand of curly hair from the side of her face. "So regimented. Don't tell me you schedule your shits too."

I did not tell her.

"Do you want to continue as Serge and Charlene now?" I said, glancing at my phone. We were already fifteen minutes into the hour.

"Nah," said Darlene. "I'm too tired today to pretend. Can we just talk or something?"

"Sure," I said. Whatever the client wanted, the client got.

"So tell me about this fake daughter of yours."

"That's confidential," I said.

"Boring," said Darlene, kicking at a loose branch in the path. "You got any real kids?"

"No," I said.

"Yeah," said Darlene. "I bet that'd complicate things too much."

"You?" I asked.

"Me what?"

"You got any real kids?"

Darlene laughed, aiming for the shoulder but punching me in the elbow. "No way," she said. "Don't want 'em either."

"Why not?" I asked, even though it was abundantly clear—from the way she dressed to how her hair could break any brush that dared tango with it—that she could barely take care of herself, much less another living being.

Darlene rubbed at her nose, suddenly quiet. "That's confidential," she said.

"Fair," I said, despite finding myself uncharacteristically curious.

"I could never be a mother," said Darlene, "but I could be an aunt." She winked. "Fun, kooky Aunt Darlene! She has five pet tarantulas and is unemployed but calls herself a writer—stay in school, kiddo, and don't major in English or anthropology or you might end up like her!"

As we wound our way back around the park, Darlene made a spur-of-the-moment decision to challenge one of the chess players.

"You play?" she asked.

"No," I said. I had neither the desire nor the opportunity to play chess, but envisioned I would be pretty good at the game. A few years ago, a woman hired me to accompany her to a renaissance fair, where we watched a life-sized game of chess play out, the pieces dressed as their respective sixteenth-century counterparts. It was a war turned board game turned war game. Watching the players move, I easily grasped the heart of chess. It was similar to my strategy on the job: predict the movements of others, then take control by limiting their options. If you force the rules of the encounter, you win. Executed correctly, my job could be as beautifully played as a game of chess. But still, we each had our lanes. The Union Square guys could never do what I did, and I would never challenge them to a match; the key to winning a game of chess or playing a rental role perfectly was repetition, and these guys played more games in a day than I changed names.

Darlene sat down as the chess shark offered her the white pieces and the first turn. I was surprised by the amount of time she took to ponder each move, her eyes darting back and forth across the eight-by-eight grid. Her match lasted longer than those around her, but after a while she looked up at me and said, "Time's up, isn't it?"

I nodded.

She moved her bishop to take a knight and smiled, saying, "Good match."

"But it's not over," said the chess shark.

"Oh, I'm going to lose in ten turns," said Darlene, still smiling. "Good game though. Here's a twenty, keep the change."

The man sized her up, surprised by how confident she was in her own inevitable defeat, but then returned to his hustle. "You next?" he said.

I shook my head. I wasn't in the business of throwing money away; besides, I had another client to get to.

"See you next time," said Darlene. "I'll text you."

"Please don't," I said, but without conviction, as Darlene skipped away, waving goodbye without a backward glance.

For the rest of the afternoon, I went on a date where a young man reminisced about the great restaurants in Melbourne, and then later, in the early evening, I went on a walk with an older woman, regaling her in an Australian accent about the great restaurants of my birthplace, Melbourne. I advertised a few accents on my profile: Southern, British, Scottish, pan-Scandinavian, pan-Asian, Korean (the easiest of the Asian accents to pick up), Japanese (slightly harder), and Australian. An accent, of course, cost extra, but I found that many of my female clients would shell out for British or Australian accents. Korean accents were also becoming more popular among the younger crowd. Personally, the accents helped me get into character, as though a whole life could be shaped by the way I pronounced my *rs*.

Back at home, I shelved my shoes on a rack and righted a vacuum cleaner that had toppled over. The sun was tucking itself behind the skyline earlier and earlier these days, and an orange glow backlit my menus, reminding me that I was hungry. Thai food was top of mind as I'd been gushing over the best chicken satays in Oz while strolling the Ramble, though now I would have to settle for the best within a ten-block radius. In reality, outside of one cross-country flight from LA to NYC, the only travel I'd ever done was in my unlived lives.

After brushing my teeth, I practiced Darlene's smile from the end of the chess match in the mirror in order to use it on others when I wanted to make them wonder if I'd predicted the outcome all along. I felt maliciously joyful—like a cat watching a songbird, aware of the very timbre of its dying note before the sound even tickled the bird's throat.

Back in bed, under my incandescent lighting, I prepared myself for who I would need to be tomorrow. As I scrolled through international import-export terminology, a message popped up from Darlene.

Have a good night!

I began to type a response about not using this service like texting but then deleted it. What an exhausting woman, I thought.

Good night, I wrote back.

That night, I dreamed I'd lost Lily in a crowd of people who knew that I was a fraud, and so they hid her from me, the multitude crashing against me like embodied waves, determined to drag me out to sea. I tried to protest, to say that I meant no harm, that I was doing it for her happiness, but her keepers snarled and snapped like rabid dogs. When one woman, with long black hair and a familiar beauty mark on her cheek, clawed at my eyes, darkening my vision, I jolted awake to find that my apartment was blackout black. I never turned off my lights. A power outage.

I was painfully aware of my heart thudding an escape from its bony cage and I shut my eyes, knocking over the stack of books that made up my nightstand as I grasped for my phone. It's fine—I reminded myself—everything is fine, you live alone, there's no one here, you live alone, you are alone, nothing has happened. I scooped my phone from the ground and turned on the flashlight, which cast long shadows from the clutter of my boxes and clothes.

"Nothing nothing nothing no one no one no one," I muttered to myself. I surveyed my palms, clean. Heartbeat still irregular, I rearranged my book nightstand and propped my phone up so that I could fall asleep to a lit room, but sleep eluded me. I couldn't shake the feeling that beyond the reach of light, at the border of dream and memory, someone waited for me to find her in the shadowed dark.

CHAPTER 12

Mari leaned against the railing of the stoop as she smoked a cigarette. I stood facing her, shivering in my light jacket. After a dinner of egg-and-tomato stir-fry, Lily had been put to bed, and Mari had said she wanted to talk, so I followed her outside. Though the sun had already set, residual light still wine-stained the sky a light purple. We both waited, watching Mari's smoke drift upward, past streetlights and redbrick buildings and into the night air.

"Listen," she said, "I think I'm gonna have to go back to these team happy hours; otherwise my boss won't be happy."

I doubted this forced socialization was legal, but what could I say? It wasn't my place to meddle in Mari's life. The red glow at the end of her cigarette deepened the soft pouches beneath her eyes. No one could say that this woman didn't work hard to pay for the illusion of a stable family for her daughter.

She sighed. "What do you think?"

"About what?"

"Like, should I go drinking with the boss or not?"

Ash stirred at her feet. I knew what Lily would want: what

every child—what I had—wanted. In elementary and middle school, on my long walks back home, where I'd imagine gargantuan monsters climbing over duplexes and dingbat apartments, and I, depending on my mood, would either run from them or blast them away. Somewhere in the back of my mind I hoped that upon opening the front door to whichever apartment we happened to live in at the time, my mother would be there—reading a script so intently that she hadn't realized the light outside was fading. More often than not, though, I returned home to an empty, darkening room. I had a rule that if I hadn't stepped on any cracks in the sidewalk the whole way back and then touched the doorknob three times before opening the front door, she would be there. I can't remember if this worked or not—I always inadvertently stepped on cracks.

I couldn't tell Mari how to parent Lily. It had gone over horribly last time. Yet I wanted us to be a unit, much like we had been in the earlier years. I tried to convey this in the language of money, in which Mari was fluent.

"If you do go," I said, "you'd have to add on a few hours to the recurring scheduler, so with that in mind—"

"Is that all we are to you?" said Mari, biting down on her cigarette. "Money?"

I was surprised by her response. Wasn't this the way we'd always communicated? Speaking in dollars and cents, hours and minutes as shorthand? I thought she knew that I rarely actually considered money when thinking of them. Instead, I thought about the way she and I used to casually chat over dinner and whisper our goodbyes after Lily had gone to bed, about how she used to call me Prince Charming (when had that stopped?), about how much I hated the idea of a man with hairy knuckles passing Mari one drink after another until she couldn't make judgments that were the best for her daughter, for her family, for us.

She stubbed the cigarette out on the railing. "It feels like I've been falling into my own trap these days. I forgot who I'm talking to. But that's my fault. It's not like I'm paying you to give me advice."

"I'm sorry," I said. "I think you misunderstood."

"Oh yeah?" said Mari.

"What I meant was: I want to make sure that you and Lily are happy," I said. And then, surprising myself with the force of my own conviction, "So don't go drinking with the boss if you can't afford to."

Mari laughed mirthlessly, but then she smiled, tilting her head to look at me. "You know we can't afford shit," she said. "Can barely afford you."

We stood, Mari leaning against the wall, and me standing a few paces away from her, both of us looking out over the emptying streets.

"Got cold," Mari said.

"I'll let you go back inside," I said, taking that as my cue to leave. I blew into my cupped hands for warmth.

To my surprise, Mari took two swift steps forward and gave me a hug. The top of her head, which came up to my chest, smelled of smoke and citrus. I resisted the urge to clear my throat. I'd been embraced before by clients, but only ever while playing a role, which meant that I'd expected it. Despite playing a married couple, Mari and I rarely touched. During Christmas I might make a show of kissing Mari on the cheek for Lily's sake, but even then my lips only hovered, close enough to smell the department store perfume she'd sprayed from her sample bottle, but not close enough to feel her skin beneath my lips. The hug caught me especially off guard because it was happening after work hours—meaning that it wasn't for Lily's sake but for me, for my sake. When was the last time I'd been held so close?

"Thanks," she said.

"Everything will be okay," I said into Mari's hair.

I could feel her nodding against my chest. My whole body felt warm, and in that moment, I knew that this job was what I was meant to be doing. Mari and Lily would be pivotal to my redemption. I could say the words now that I should have said back then, to my mother. "It'll all be okay. Everything will work out," I said, with a head rush so intense that my voice echoed in my own ears. "I promise."

Mari's face was inscrutable in the rapidly fading light, but she held on tight as though I were a life raft. We parted ways with a whispered good night.

After the door to her building swung shut, I stood on the stoop a minute longer, my skin tingling with residual warmth. It felt like static shock, the scratch of her wool jacket and the friction of her arms around me. I could be dependable this time. I wouldn't fail again.

CHAPTER 13

My mother was my whole life, until she wasn't. Though she'd been an actress, when we moved to New York for what was supposed to be her big break, instead she was often writing, typing late into the night. Yet when she died, there was no sign of her work—her laptop was missing and the printed pages lashed with handwritten comments had disappeared. The only writing she left behind was a single sticky note that said "Forgive Me," but what was I supposed to forgive her for?

She was a stunning woman, tall, with long black hair and hooded eyes that seemed to know exactly what you were thinking. She had a beauty mark high on her left cheek that I found out later in life was drawn on. Mother often felt like that: a slippery presence, a mirage in the desert that, from time to time, ended up being a real oasis where you could sit down, cool off, and drink. So how to explain her? Maybe it's possible only in fits and starts.

My earliest memories of my mother are sonic—lines repeated day and night, punctuated by a lid rattling atop a pot of boiling liquid that spilled over the sides. Even now I can hear her, reciting lines to the sizzle of steam as moisture hit the electric coil. I was around twenty when I realized that boiling water didn't require an overflow.

During my childhood, we moved from apartment to apartment in different neighborhoods around LA, and I remember the anticipation of uncovering secret passageways or false walls (I was a child fed on fantasy) in these places. Never finding any, I decided to hide myself instead. In our Chinatown apartment, I hid beneath beds and inside boiler closets, in part to add some drama to my life, and in part to test whether my mother could tell I was missing. I wanted to see if she would worry the way the teacher worried when recess ended and they couldn't locate a student who'd found a winning hiding spot in hide-and-seek. I purposefully chose places that were relatively obvious, both at school and around the apartment, because the thrill of being undetected was paltry compared to the relief of being found. But unlike the schoolchildren who always located me right away, my own mother was never any good at finding me. Once, when I was seven, I fell asleep beneath the kitchen sink, and when I crawled out—shoulder radiating with the pain of being scrunched beneath the drainpipe for hours—the apartment was dark, and my mother had fallen asleep on the couch with a script held close to her chest. Her long hair slid down the sofa's arm like a waterfall, and her mouth was slightly open, as though she were surprised to be caught in such a state of disorder. Maybe she often slept out here between my hours of sleeping and waking, or maybe she was waiting for me to return home and had botched her vigil. Either way, she hadn't found me. I covered my mother with a blanket and never played hide-and-seek again.

I was an obedient kid, diligent and quiet, but when I was nine, I confronted my mother for the first time, asking her why she didn't comfort me when I was upset like parents on TV did for their children: kneeling down to their height, a hand on the shoulder, a word of support. "Comfort?" she'd said. "If I comfort you when you're upset, you'll just be upset more often to seek comfort. Why would I want you to become dependent on unhappiness?" At first I was confused by her response, but after mulling it over, it made sense. From then on, I trained myself to hide negative emotions. It worked just like she'd said: when I knew no one would comfort me, I was unhappy for a shorter amount of time. I learned how to take care of myself. With this new perspective, I could see how many other people chose to wallow in the stink of their own misery as they waited (sometimes unknowingly) for a helping hand; though I pitied them, I did not judge. Instead, I guided them, leading them out of the muck into clean waters to wash. But I'm afraid I'm showing my mother in too harsh a light—she was not a monster. Whenever I was truly upset, she drove me up the winding roads of PCH in our old Corolla, the back windows that wouldn't close all the way funneling a vortex of wind past my ears that made my head pulse. The sensation was unbearable, but because of that, I couldn't think of anything else, not even what had upset me in the first place. My physical discomfort displaced everything. One time, we made it as far north as Big Sur, and after a minute of craning our necks up at the ageless trees that made us feel too small, we drove home.

One final anecdote, though this one is a bit embarrassing. In high school, we moved to and stayed in Westlake the longest I'd stayed anywhere, so I had the time to develop a massive crush on a girl the year above me. She had shiny black hair and wit like a revolver, always another retort readied in the chamber. Seeking direction in the ways of funny, I studied the humorous writers in my mother's collection (when the librarians complained of my mother's "handling" of books, she began her own collection, purchased from street-side peddlers selling paperbacks for a dollar)—Wilde, Austen, Spark. But every time I had the chance to speak with this girl, all I could ever manage was "huh!" and "hah!" like I possessed a single Neanderthaloid brain cell. When junior year rolled around, I gathered up my resolve to ask her to prom, but I was missing a key component.

"I need a suit," I said, sitting at the kitchen table as my mother gathered up our empty dinner bowls.

"Who died?" said Mother.

"What?"

"If you're not attending a funeral, why would we need a suit?" *We* didn't need a suit—I wanted to tell her—*I* needed a suit. Mother had always posited possessions as ours, as though we could split a pair of shoes, a jacket, slacks, and a tie between us (though I had, at one point, been fascinated with my mother's shoes and dresses, but outgrew that, in both senses of the word). This verbal tic of hers had never bothered me before that day, but from then on it bothered me incessantly, though it wasn't until we moved to New York that things got really bad. At least in our parts of LA, miserliness was normal— all the kids I went to school with were also borderline broke. Though the internet had introduced us to LA wealth, those were always *other* people—they weren't my classmates—and anyway, we were better than them. We were real. We made fun of the plastic men and women of Hollywood, betting that their genitals were smooth as a doll's. In New York City, however, wealth couldn't even give poor people like me the courtesy of being easily mocked. Money hid itself. You never knew you were talking to the daughter of a multi-millionaire until she decided to fly to Warsaw for a weekend when you could barely afford a can of soda to go with your cafeteria lunch. As I confronted this harsh reality with no brothers-in-arms to turn to, the loathing moved inward, and then exploded against the person unfortunate enough to be near me—my mother. At first I'd pestered her about why we couldn't also get away for the summer ("Get away from what?" she'd asked), or when I'd get the latest Nikes ("when you stop asking"), or why she wasn't hitting it big-time when we'd uprooted our whole life for that purpose (silence). After the first few months in Bed-Stuy, my rage spent, I stopped talking to her at all, stopped going to school, stopped caring about anything except how to best waste time, make a quick dollar, or fuck the Medgar Evers girl who thought I was in college too.

But I'm losing the thread; junior prom was before all that—before I'd ever had a nipple in my mouth that I hadn't suckled as a babe.

"I'm in love!" I'd said to my mother, stupidly, without thinking. At the time, I was pretty sure I was in love. The requisite butterflies in my stomach were working overtime, I could pick her voice out in a crowded auditorium, and I could sense without looking when she was within a fifty-foot radius of me. "I want to ask her to prom so I need a suit."

My mother said nothing in response to my outburst, placing the dishes in the sink and pulling on her yellow rubber gloves.

"Mom!" I shouted.

She began washing the bowls. Oftentimes, my mother preferred to be left alone with her thoughts; she signaled this by acting as though I weren't there. I figured this might have been one of those times, but I was beginning to tire of always following her moods, wants, and whims. Irritation ripping through me, I pushed my chair out and it skipped on the linoleum.

Without turning around, my mother spoke. "Let's say the three of us were scuba diving in the ocean," she said, "me, you, and this person you think you love. We're swimming in murky waters. Suddenly, a shark appears. You are the only one with a knife. Who would you stab and leave as bait so that the other person could get away?"

Taken aback, I watched my mother's narrow shoulder blades move like vestigial wings beneath her T-shirt as she scrubbed.

"I'd—I'd stab the shark."

"You can't do that," she said, turning to face me as the plate in her hand drip-dripped suds to the floor. "You have to choose. Who would you stab?" My mother, with that drawn-on mark on her cheek, watching me, waiting for an answer. Could she see it? The answer in my heart?

"Her, I guess," I said.

"Well then," said my mother, "maybe you're not in love after all."

It was an unnerving conversation. I never ended up asking the girl to prom. How could I? I didn't have the costume or the conviction necessary to play the part. Sometimes I wondered if I had answered my mother's question truthfully, whether she'd noticed a wavering. Was that the real reason why we'd left California? Because whatever big break she'd thought was coming in New York never came.

Looking back now, there isn't anyone I wouldn't kill in order to save my mother. To see her again. To ask her how and where and why she got the gun. Had I made her so desperately unhappy in New York that there was no other choice but to wrap her hands around a weapon not just sufficient to kill, but almost guaranteed when used at close range to cause injury so irreversible that it doesn't give her child who opened the door to a darkened (dark, so very dark) home even a splinter of a chance to try to stanch the bleeding and then fumble with a phone that won't open with his fingerprint because his fingers are slick with blood, until finally he manages to press and hold down the emergency call button just to answer a series of inane questions about whether the victim is male or female, and how many people are in the dark, dark room, and please describe in detail what is happening, because by then the je ne sais the fuck quoi of what makes a human alive is undoubtedly gone from the body still clutching the gun, which fired a bullet that traveled at twice the speed of sound, meaning that she probably didn't even hear the gunshot that ended her life, but she knew, before her existence flickered out, that she wanted everything to be over, while you, who she left behind, had no idea she wanted everything to be over, until you saw the hole in her chest, and now you can never ask why? And you'll never hear her say your name again.

*

I lied, one last story. My mother and I witnessed our first snowfall in New York City not long after she'd dragged a raging teenager across the country. She had been so enchanted by the flurries that she rushed outside, and I—determined to do the opposite of her— stayed indoors, my back turned to the windows, refusing to acknowledge the swirling eddies of white. Later, as I cleaned out our fridge after her suicide, I discovered that she had collected several cups of snow to stow in the freezer. In one of them was a frozen mouse, its forepaws in front of its face, eyes wide open and fingers splayed as though shielding itself from disaster. By then, the snow had become solid chunks of ice with no memory of soft, delicate flakes.

CHAPTER 14

Darlene and I met up again on a Tuesday afternoon. This time she insisted that I play the sister character and she be the brother. She was surprisingly good at it—a bit overly sloppy, but loving and charming in a way that made you think, maybe the drinking isn't so bad if it softens his edges like this.

"Bravo," I said, applauding her performance at the end.

"Gracias," she said with a mock bow, "I learned from the best."

"You flatter me," I said.

"How's my niece doing?" said Darlene.

I shook my head. "Hopefully forgetting about her phantom aunt."

"That's too bad," said Darlene, "written out before I was even written in."

The problem, though, was that Lily hadn't forgotten about her aunt. In fact, she was finding every opportunity to slyly ask about her newfound relative. I should have recognized that Lily—who had no family aside from her mother and father, and who craved the aunties and uncles and cousins and dogs that other people took for granted, especially around the holiday season—would not let extended family go very easily. I was the same way too, when I was younger: always hoping that someone—a grandparent, an uncle, maybe even my father—would walk through our front door and liven up our home that was only ever visited by fictional characters my mother and I rehearsed.

"She's doing okay," I said, wiping down a spot on the counter I'd already cleaned.

"Can I see her?" said Lily.

"Probably not," I said. "She's leaving New York soon."

"Is that why she wanted to see you?"

"Exactly."

"Can we see her before she goes?"

"I don't know . . ."

"I'm sure you could convince her. You're very convincing!"

It wasn't like Lily to wheedle and bargain; usually a single "no" was enough.

"I'll ask," I said, acknowledging her efforts without any intention of actually asking.

"You promise?" said Lily.

"Yup," I said.

"Pinky promise?"

I looped her pinky in mine and we pressed thumbs. This gesture, as binding as anything for a nine-year-old, satisfied her. No further mention was made of the elusive relative that day.

The following afternoon, the source of my aunt troubles was ranting about how she would establish herself in the New York literary scene so that her classmates would finally understand themselves to be the misguided queefs-for-brains they so obviously were. Workshop that week had not gone well, and her deadline was looming. Darlene was in no mood to be anyone but herself as she gesticulated wildly, slurping Shandong noodles from a black plastic container.

We sat in sticky low-backed chairs in a narrow, cash-only noodle restaurant where the menu was plastered onto the wall with half an inch of stickers indicating price increases over the years. The authenticity of the restaurant, recently touted on social media, had since changed. Rather than beer-bellied men picking at their teeth with toothpicks, and middle-aged women with tight perms complaining about those men to each other (or to those men's faces) in regional dialects of Mandarin, the restaurant was packed with young, hip New Yorkers blithely chattering on in English. It astounded me, the way these kids could claim any space like it belonged to them. Even I, as half-white, felt like I was intruding with my clumsy tongue that tripped over itself trying to properly pronounce the tones for 面条.

"Damn, I've been talking nonstop, huh," said Darlene, mouth full of half-chewed noodles. "This must get boring for you. I mean, what's it like always considering other people's feelings before your own? Do you only do it, like, when you're working, or do you always do it? I mean, does it come naturally?"

I nudged boiled dumplings around my Styrofoam plate. Truthfully, I wasn't naturally considerate or kind. This demeanor was practiced and controlled, a paid act, an atonement for driving my mother to the end of her life. I knew that a thousand acts of kindness wouldn't bring my mother back—but what else could I do? I couldn't forget her, and I couldn't forgive myself.

Since Darlene didn't need to know any of this, I demurred with a joke.

"Putting others above myself comes half-naturally," I said, "since I'm half-Asian."

Darlene flushed, the color creeping upward from her chest like a red turtleneck. "That's not," she said, "I would never—"

"That wasn't a submissive Asian comment?"

"Not funny," said Darlene, gripping her chopsticks tightly. "Micro-aggressions are not cool and that was not what I was saying. Don't put words in my mouth."

"I'm kidding," I said. "Jokes."

Darlene leaned her chair back but stopped when she realized there were only four inches of space between her and the person behind her. "I marched in the Stop Asian Hate rallies, you know."

"That's good," I said. And it was good, solidarity, but the only way I knew how to handle race was the way my friends in LA and I talked about it—through jokes. Somehow, we all tacitly agreed there was no point to further discussion. What was there to gain from me talking about my experiences or you yours? I would never be a white woman, and Darlene would never live my life.

"My family was persecuted during the war," said Darlene, "on my mom's side—Polish Jews. Bet you didn't know I was Jewish, huh?"

"I'm sorry," I said, and I was sorry—sorry that I'd ever brought up the topic of race. "I'm from the West Coast so it's hard for me to tell the difference between Jewish and white people," I said, trying to bring us back to light-hearted territory, though, in my estimation, if your skin tone blended in with the Upper East Side crowd and your nose bridge could hold up a pair of glasses, you were white. I thought Darlene might find this line of thinking irreverent enough to be funny, but though she possessed more self-awareness than most people, this topic had hit a nerve.

"Wow," Darlene said, digging around in her poncho for her wallet. "Wow." She paid for our meal in cash. I was worried she might cancel the rest of our time together, but instead we walked around Chinatown in silence, stopping at a boba joint. I kicked myself for going too far with my ribbing. Strange as she was, I enjoyed the hours we spent together—though I certainly wouldn't admit it aloud.

Before parting ways, I tried to make things right. "Sorry about what I said earlier. It was in poor taste."

"That's okay," said Darlene. "I know I look white as fuck."

"There's nothing wrong with that," I said, though why I was consoling someone for looking too white was unclear.

"Do you think," she said, digging for the remaining boba with her straw, "that means I can't write about non-white characters?"

"I guess we never discussed what race your characters are."

"Well, Serge is Asian," said Darlene.

I nodded. It made sense now, why she'd chosen me as a rental. There weren't as many Asian rentals as there were of other races, especially male rentals.

"And his sister?"

"Adopted, Black Jew."

"Why does she need to be Black?"

"I don't know," said Darlene, beginning to look panicked. "I wanted her to be, like, an outsider?" Darlene bit at her boba straw. "She's also a lesbian."

"And you're?"

"I've considered it?"

"Um."

"Right, okay." The straw squeaked against its plastic lid as she yanked it out and in with her teeth. "Oh my God, did I just make my characters a Benetton ad for underrepresentation? This is a problem, isn't it? But I can't make all my characters white or white-passing Jews, can I? That seems problematic too."

I didn't answer, confident that she could arrive at the correct conclusion herself.

"Damn, I gotta go," said Darlene. "I can't turn this in to my advisor, shit shit shit."

"Good luck," I said, and I meant it. In the past I'd played roles that required me to be Costa Rican or South African, but in those roles I was still Asian–Costa Rican or white–South African—even my made-up roles had natural limits. But was writing a person not the same color as you equivalent to an actor smearing on dark paint or taping up the corners of his eyes? Luckily, it wasn't my question to ponder.

I wandered west through the tunneling streets of lower Manhattan back to my apartment, picking up a costume along the way for a Halloween party upstate in about a week's time.

Thanks 4 helping me not get canceled lol, read a message from Darlene as I reached the entrance of my building.

"Ohh," said one of the guys in front of my apartment, the one with the self-valued expensive watch. "Text from the girlfriend? I see that smile! You should bring her home sometime. Meet the family," he said, gesturing to the five or so guys lining the street, one of them sitting on what looked like an office swivel chair.

"It's work," I said, not realizing I'd been smiling.

"Ah-ah," he said, "poor American, married to his work! Work won't keep you warm at night. What you need is the love of a woman."

I laughed, jamming my key into the door and jiggling it open. A woman's love? What would that even feel like? Oppressive? Sweet? The guy drew deep from his vape and the smoke he blew my way smelled of lemons. I wondered, for a moment before opening the door, what Mari was doing on a Friday evening.

CHAPTER 15

Over the course of a few days, the temperature had plunged from the seventies to the forties. As I returned from a job walking around Central Park with an elderly Polish woman, the yellowing leaves reminded me of Lily's mustard-colored coat that her mother had bought her last fall. Like Lily's worn skirts and shirts, the coat was now well beyond its natural lifespan. She had grown a few inches since last fall, so I could already envision the snaps down the middle struggling to clasp together, sleeves landing too short above her wrists. My head bent down against the wind that was picking up on Canal Street, I noticed in my peripheral vision a flash of teal. Pop-up boutiques had set up shop in the previously shuttered storage units lining my side of Canal Street, and one of them was now selling children's clothes. On display was a teal-blue jacket with a white faux-fur lining that would be perfect for Lily, bringing out the blue-black of her hair and lighting up her eyes. Other pedestrians nearly bumped into me while I stood captivated in the middle of the sidewalk, but like good New Yorkers, they cursed and then quickly flowed around my sides like I was a rock in their stream.

I'd purchased items for clients before, but only at their request, and I was reimbursed right away. I knew Mari would never ask me to buy anything for her daughter nor could she afford to reimburse a boutique item, but surely even Mari would understand that Lily needed new outerwear this season or else her overexposed wrists would chafe in the cold. Maybe I could convince Lily to tell her mom that it had been a birthday present from a classmate. Hopefully she remembered the lesson on necessary lies.

Inside, I found the jacket on a rack and passed it to the salesclerk, a young woman with green highlights in her hair, who informed me that she'd designed the coat herself. She made children's clothing because she couldn't conceive; her designs were odes to the children she would never have. The garments in the store did have a touch of whimsy to them, like outfits only imaginary happy children could wear. I nodded along until she rang up the jacket for $240, and I realized that I hadn't checked the price tag before bringing it up to the counter. It had felt so transgressive to buy Lily a gift in the first place that I'd snatched it up as quickly as possible. This would be by far the largest expenditure I'd made outside of my rent—most of my clothing and costuming was charged to wealthy clients and what I'd bought for myself was always at bargain prices. The clerk/designer noted my hesitation and informed me that the jacket was handmade and worth every cent and, in fact, considering the labor involved in birthing it (her words, not mine), might even be worth more than the price tag indicated. I had a little nest egg saved up and could afford the jacket, but I still needed a moment to recover from the sticker shock. I quickly handed over my credit card as the clerk drummed her paint-chipped nails on the counter. I told her it was, indeed, a beautiful work of art, asked her to cut the tag off, and then left with the jacket stuffed in a paper bag.

During the train ride uptown, the heater was broken and I could not stop shivering. I shoved my balled-up fists into the fur lining of Lily's new coat. It was warm, and the stitching, I could feel, was carefully done and wouldn't unravel as easily as the rest of her clothes.

The school bell rang right as I arrived at the gates, and kids of all ages began to trickle out. Usually, Lily was the first one out the door, but today a full parade of other children came before her. It was astonishing how many different types of kids there were: squat kids, spry kids, spongey kids, sulky kids, so many variations that, over time, would get stamped into the proper shape for adult life—harried and hardened. Eventually, when all the parents picking up children had left and the only kids hanging around were playing handball against the school wall or sitting around playing on their cell phones, in no rush to go anywhere, I started to worry that something might have happened to Lily. Should I go into the school and speak with someone? I'd never been inside, and I wasn't sure whose name was registered in the spot for Lily's father. I doubted that elementary schools took kindly to strange men asking after prepubescent girls. Right as I was about to call Mari, I saw Lily coming out the door with a young boy, tight curls cut close to his head and high cheeks that hardened into round chestnuts when he smiled. He and Lily were holding hands and I gripped the handles of my bag tighter. Lily dropped the boy's hand when she saw me. He tried to pick it back up but she shooed him away.

"Everything okay?" I said, taking a few wide strides to reach her.

The boy, oblivious to Lily's embarrassment, mimicked my stride and stuck his hand up toward me. He took a deep breath. "Hello Mr. Tanaka I'm Piri Torrez Jr. Lily's boyfriend it's nice to meet you." The way he introduced himself reminded me of the way I used to introduce myself when I first started off as a Rental Stranger, before I'd learned how to be comfortable in my borrowed skin. From the strain in the bottom corners of his mouth (a genuine smile would lift from the top) and the flare of his little nostrils, I could tell that he was anxious to make a good first impression. I recognized the name Piri as the boy Lily had brought up at Grand Central: the object of Lily's desire who'd once made fun of her nose. Though I was surprised by this new development, I realized I shouldn't have been; after all, as a young boy, I too had teased the girls I liked in the hope that they would notice me. It didn't matter how I got her attention—as bully or buffoon—if she looked my way, my day shone that much brighter. No one had taught me, or Piri, it seemed, how to behave otherwise around the person we wanted to like us most. I felt a small kinship for this scrawny kid and shook his hand—he had a strong grip, so at least that was good.

"Nice to meet you, Piri," I said. "And how long have you two been, ah, together?"

"About a week, sir," said Piri. "I've been walking her home from school."

"That's very gentlemanly of you," I said, and Piri beamed, a real smile this time, his cheeks squeezing his eyes to crescents. I wanted to ask Lily why her mother wasn't picking her up from school, but I doubted Lily knew the answer to that. Maybe she was simply old enough to walk home alone now. I wished Mari had mentioned this new development to me, but there was no rule that she had to. At the very least I could be grateful to Piri that Lily had company. "I'll take Lily home today," I said.

"Actually," said Lily, taking two of my fingers in her hand, "I told Piri he could come over to study since his Abuelo isn't going to be home until late."

I had guessed that Piri's guardians, like mine as a child, were largely absent, but my sympathy could extend only so far. Had Piri also been staying at the apartment with Lily this past week until her mother arrived? What exactly did they do alone, together? Those times I'd visited friends' places after school there was always a mother or uncle or grandfather or older sister or younger brother or second cousin or all of the above; the one time I'd taken a friend back to my quiet apartment in Watts, the kid had knocked over a stack of papers and my mother, upon returning home, coolly told me to never invite anyone to our place ever again. And that was that.

On our walk, Lily held on to my hand and Piri, who didn't quite know where to stand, would at times position himself in front of us or beside us, all the while chattering about the latest shoot-em-up games or their gassy teacher. I wondered what Lily saw in this kid, whose interests were more akin to a typical ten-year-old's than to Lily's, but when she openly laughed at his antics, I began to understand why a serious little girl might be attracted to someone who thought fart jokes were apex humor.

We passed by men sitting on stools, smoking and snacking in front of the cell phone repair/key replicator/shoe cobbler/hardware store whose tiny window was more packed with merchandise and sales posters than commuters on the 6 train at 4 p.m. on a Friday afternoon. Piri waved hi, revealing that one of the guys was his uncle. Most of the parents in Lily's school worked at small businesses like this or helped run greasy spoon restaurants. As a long-haul truck driver, I afforded Lily some cred among the kids. When Piri asked if he could see my truck, I said that it was parked outside the city, and both he and Lily were visibly disappointed.

"But look, I got you a present!" I said to Lily, holding out the paper bag. She was wearing, as I'd suspected, the yellow jacket from previous years, with barely enough coverage to withstand the gusts of the late fall, much less the winter.

"Oh oh!" said Piri. "It's for her birthday!" he exclaimed, excited to prove what he knew about her, as though memorizing biodata was tantamount to love.

"Happy belated birthday," I said.

Lily reached inside and pulled out the jacket.

"Wow," she said, holding it up gently, precious as a newborn, "it's amazing."

"Put it on!" said Piri, almost as excited as Lily was.

She struggled to strip off the old, overly tight coat, but the new, turquoise jacket slid on easily, and she looked like a girl transformed—the sheen of the waterproof exterior juxtaposed with the pure white of the fur trim transported her to the spread of a children's magazine. Piri, meanwhile, in his polyester windbreaker with dinosaur print, was the kid flipping through its pages, dreaming of a life his parents could not afford. I'm not sure if Piri understood this or felt it instinctively, but something in his face changed as soon as Lily smiled, delighted in the jacket's embrace. He crossed his scrawny arms.

"You kinda look like a whale," he said, "all blue and stuff."

An ambulance screamed past us and Lily's face fell. She fingered the fur on the hood carefully so as not to get it dirty. Slowly, she shrugged the jacket off. "Thanks, Dad," she said, "but I'll wear the other one for now." Any goodwill I'd had toward Piri evaporated. I wanted to smack this kid, but I was more hurt by Lily's unwillingness to wear the coat. The jacket was so expensive; if she didn't wear it now she might outgrow it. Wasteful, I thought, as I stuffed it back into the bag. My mother would not have tolerated such wastefulness.

In the apartment stairwell, Lily took the stairs one at a time while Piri demonstrated how he could skip a step if he jumped far enough. When he nicked the edge of the stair at the fifth-floor landing and started falling backward, propelling his arms like he could swim himself through the air and back up to vertical, I hesitated only a split second before catching him by the shoulders.

"Oh," he said quietly, scrambling to right himself and then stuffing his hands beneath his armpits to preserve his masculine pride, but when he saw that Lily was opening the door to the apartment and hadn't noticed his gaffe, he shook his head and wiped his sweating palms on the front of his jeans. "Thanks, Mr. T," he said. It took me a second to remember that T stood for Tanaka.

Inside, the two kids plunked down at the dining room table, which had two matching chairs and one bought later when I joined the family. I wondered if Lily ever noticed this mismatch, and if she didn't before, would she now when viewing her home through Piri's eyes? Would she notice, also, that there were nearly no signs of me in this household? My clothes were not in the drawers, my shoes not in the closet. I didn't even have a toothbrush in the plastic cup on the bathroom sink. But I wanted Piri to see how comfortable I was in this space, so as they tackled their homework, I vacuumed, mopped, and wiped down the apartment, marking it by erasure.

Piri, who could not stay silent for the amount of time required to actually get homework done, wondered aloud if maybe he could have a soda. I informed him that there were no sodas in this house and that if he wanted one, he would have to go to the bodega around the corner and get it himself. Lily, perhaps to counteract my curt response, offered juice, which Piri gladly accepted. I stopped her from getting up and poured guava juice into two mugs, giving Piri the one with a slightly chipped lip.

Watching the two of them studying together—Lily's head bent over her books in deep concentration while Piri worried at a scab on his elbow, fiddled with his hair, and picked at his toes—it was obvious that she was going to outstrip this young boy in life. When she explained vocabulary words to him, I could tell from the blank expression on his face that he needed a definition of her definition but was too proud to say so. Shame that these boys developed egos at such a young age.

I wasn't so unreasonable as to assume that people couldn't or wouldn't change in the future, but these were formative years. What if during the short duration of their young romance, Piri and his insecurities shaped how Lily conducted her future relationships? What if his inability to let her enjoy what was out of his reach damaged her sense of self-worth? What if she ended up with a deadbeat like Mari's ex-boyfriend or a predator like Ajay or a fraud . . . like me? Because as bad as Piri might be for my little girl, what could he possibly do to Lily that I wasn't already laying the groundwork for? The fallout of an elementary school relationship was microwave radiation compared to the nuclear damage of discovered pretend paternity. But more and more I was warming up to the idea that there could be no damage at all. At first, in every interaction with Lily I was sure she would sniff me out for a fake because I didn't know how to be a dad. But as the years passed, and I settled into the role, I began to believe that maybe I could play a good father, and do it well enough to make Lily happy. I rarely thought of the future— that murky hypothetical problem that was easily solved by ignoring it. But what I couldn't ignore now was the memory of Mari's arms around me, needing me, and in this moment—watching Lily scrunch her nose in concentration over her textbooks—I could envision the rest of my life entwined with theirs: showing up every Thursday to her elementary, middle, and high schools (until she got embarrassed and told me to stop); video chatting with her in college; helping her move into her law school apartment; celebrating her passing the bar; giving a toast at her wedding; holding her mother's hand as Lily herself became a mother. All of this was easier to imagine than a life where I never saw where Lily's intellectual curiosity took her—law or otherwise—never knew her future family, never heard her call me Dad again.

Piri had drawn a comic in the margins of his textbook, which he showed Lily, who chuckled appreciatively but then returned to her math homework.

If politicians could feign competence and priests chastity, then why couldn't I be Lily's father until the day I died? It felt like a worthy endeavor—heavy, and therefore full of promise.

I slipped on rubber gloves and scooped a nasty mash of dirt and grease out of the sink's catch. Behind me, Piri turned the index and middle fingers of his right hand into the legs of an action hero who high-kicked his way across the valley of Piri's history textbook. While hosing down the sink, I sensed Piri staring at the odd figure I cut: six feet tall, bent slightly at the waist, with yellow dishwashing gloves, scrubbing the sides of the sink with an electric-blue sponge.

I turned around to find that he was in fact staring at me. He didn't look away. I asked if they wanted a snack or, perhaps, some more juice. He pursed his lips and looked me up and down: the gloves, the house slippers, the eagerness to please. His forehead creased. Did the men in his family act this way? Probably not. Was he going to say something about what the men in his family did? Was he going to make a comment about Asian subservience? Were kids introduced to these stereotypes so young? Was I being overly sensitive?

"We're okay," said Lily. "Thanks, Dad."

Piri finally spoke up and I braced myself for casual racism, a dig at my masculinity, or both.

"Want help?" he said.

"Oh," I said, not expecting this offer. "You want to help?"

For most people, being wrong about another's intentions is a daily occurrence they don't even realize is happening, but for the past decade I'd prided myself on being able to peer past what people said or did and into what they truly meant. So how could I have misjudged a young boy—the most transparent of all people? Was something clouding my judgment?

"Sure," I said, handing Piri a rag. "You can help wipe down the stovetop."

He did so without complaint, humming the jingle for some local injury attorneys as his small fingers maneuvered the rag into the crevices beneath the clawed pan supporters, clearly familiar with the task. When Lily finished her homework, I took both kids to the Mexican diner next door and told them they could order whatever they wanted, including guacamole. Piri ordered every possible filling, and his burrito was the size of an obese dachshund, while Lily's looked like a deflated pencil bag. Normally, she ate a lot more. Was this because of the whale comment Piri made earlier or was ten the age at which little girls started caring more about what people thought of them than what they wanted for themselves? I'd had many insecure women as clients, though I never asked when they'd started seeing themselves in the third person and judging themselves by someone else's standards. When I asked Lily if she wanted more beans or rice in her burrito, she shook her head no. She was still wearing the old jacket, too tight around her midsection.

After eating, Piri offered to pay me back with money I knew he didn't have. When I insisted it was my treat, he thanked me profusely for the meal and then said that he probably had to head home. He was a polite kid—I'd give him that—but still, not good enough for my Lily.

Inside the apartment, I grazed my fingernails along the fabric of the new jacket, hanging on a hook behind the door, its slick yet textured surface sounding like zippers. "Do you not like it?" I asked.

Lily's eyes widened. "I like it," she said.

"Why didn't you wear it?"

She bit her lip. "That's because it's so nice that I didn't want to get it dirty."

"Is that the only reason?" I asked.

She nodded, but looked away when I tried to catch her eye. Should I be happy that she'd caught on to the lesson of white lies so quickly? She was sharp, my little girl. Though it was also possible that she was telling the truth—when Lily started the fourth grade, Mari had bought her a new binder displaying an Arctic tundra and an aurora borealis on the cover that moved if you tilted it this way and that. That binder was still in its plastic wrapping as Lily continued to use her old one, duct-taped at the seams with misaligned rings that pinched the skin of her fingers from time to time. From the way she touched the jacket without touching it—fingers hovering a millimeter above the surface as though it were covered in plastic—I had a sinking feeling that my gift would suffer a similar fate.

"Moose, if your mom asks where you got it, tell her it was a birthday gift from a classmate," I said.

"Why?"

"Because, well, it's our little secret."

Lily mulled this over. "Okay, but the thing is, like, my friends don't—they're, um, their gifts are usually, like, smaller?"

Of course her friends, whose parents all made minimum wage, wouldn't be able to afford what was clearly an expensive jacket.

"Um," said Lily, "sometimes in school we'll have these assemblies where people compete and win prizes by spelling words correctly or completing math problems the fastest. I could say I won that."

"Brilliant," I said, both proud and worried by how easily Lily could spin a believable lie.

"That's what I'll tell Mom," said Lily, "but only on one condition."

"Shoot."

"I want to meet my aunt."

"Ah," I said. "I asked her and—" How could I keep playing Lily's father forever if I couldn't even grant this simple request? I needed to smooth over her suspicions by making my lie more and more believable so that even when she was thirty-one, she wouldn't think that I wasn't her real father—because, after all, she'd met her aunt. When two people were involved, it couldn't possibly be fabricated. "She said she could meet up briefly, next week. But then she's off to California."

Lily squealed like a proper ten-year-old and hugged my waist. I couldn't remember the last time she'd been this excited about anything, and I marveled, as I often did, at how just a few words could cause such elation.

CHAPTER 16

Mari looked drained when she returned home that evening, like gravity had doubled down on her shoulders, and when Lily mentioned seeing her aunt next week, Mari's frown lines deepened as she took a mechanical biteful of chicken that might as well have been gravel. After Lily went to bed, Mari opened a can of beer and sat back down at the table.

"The aunt thing," I said. "I'll take care of it. Don't worry." In the resulting silence, a normal person might have jumped in with more to say, but I was comfortable in pauses, and could wait for as long as Mari needed to respond. The refrigerator whined and settled. A creak and muffled laugh from the apartment across the wall. Mari slid the can around in the condensation on the table.

"I think I'm gonna lose my job," she said. "The boss isn't happy about my 'lack of team spirit.'"

I knew Mari wanted me to say something—to assure her that her boss wouldn't fire her over something so petty when she'd been a loyal worker for so long, to question the legality of such a move, or even just to call him an asshole—but I was at a loss for words. I was the one who'd told her to skip the happy hours, promising her that everything would be okay. That we'd make it work. But I hadn't expected this. Mari, jobless? What was the value of my words if she didn't have a job? Couldn't pay for my time?

"How long do you think we can keep this up for?" she said, as though reading my doubts.

The timing could not have been worse; I'd only just understood that helping Mari and Lily would help me set things right. But I couldn't tell Mari that, not without scaring her into thinking I wanted more from them than they could give. They didn't need to give me anything—I was the one who needed to give, and give, and give. "As long as you want," I said.

"Did you ever think it was weird? Our arrangement?"

"No." Though the only other times I'd played a father figure, either the child was too young to care or I was only hired for a day. It felt worse in some ways to play father for only a day, especially to a child who knew I wasn't their real dad—and who might begin to hope that I could be, only to never see me again. One little boy in particular, whose mother hired me to be a husband/father during her college reunion, wouldn't stop crying when we parted ways at the end of the night—screaming "Daddy! Daddy!" as his mother dragged him home. This was four years ago, and I had avoided these types of parent roles ever since (unless, of course, they paid handsomely). That child must be a teenager by now; I hoped he'd long forgotten about me.

"Have you ever thought about how this would end?" said Mari.

In the beginning I'd assumed Mari would have called it off long before Lily could remember me: that I'd become a pleasant haze of Father from her past, memorable as one's own first word or first steps. But now here we were, eight years later. Maybe this would be a good time to tell Mari what I'd realized: that it never had to end.

That I could be Lily's father long term. But I hesitated. Was that what Mari wanted? Or was bringing this up her way of hinting that now was a good end point for the relationship, before the situation became truly intractable? Yes, I could walk Lily down the aisle with tears in my eyes, but then what? Would Mari hand me a check at the end for working the wedding overtime? And if I stayed on indefinitely, did that mean at some point Lily would begin caring for me instead of the other way around—driving me to medical checkups when I was injured or visiting me at the nursing home? Would Mari, in her old age, pay for those visits too? Would I pay her? What did I know about being a father long term anyway?

"It's up to you," I said, backtracking. It was my advice that had gotten us into this sticky situation, after all. I defaulted to what I knew best: always give the customer what they wanted. I laid my hands on the table, palms up. "I'll do whatever makes you happy, guaranteed."

A cockroach scurried out from beneath the oven and, after doing a quick round on the kitchen tiles, scampered back to its warm, dark abode. Mari didn't notice; she was looking out the kitchen window, as though the answers to her problems roamed out there, just beyond reach.

"It's weird," she said, "how you can make me feel lonelier than when I'm alone."

"I'm sorry," I said, knowing that she wanted more from me, but Prince Charming was a coward—scared of saying the wrong thing. Afraid of blood in the water. He had a track record, after all, of hurting the people he cared about. "If you just tell me what you need, I can be more—"

"No," she said. "It's *because* you can't be more than you are. And what you are is good for Lily, but I'm realizing now—well, I don't think it's good for me."

"What can I do better?"

"Nothing," she said. "I don't want to be selfish. I don't matter. But if I'm out of a job . . . I guess I'm starting to see how dangerous this all is. How tumorous."

I nodded, thinking that maybe she meant *tumultuous* or *tenuous*, but *tumorous* worked too. Was it time? Did she want to excise me? At this point, who was I clinging on for, me or them? A barking dog nearby set off a series of yips and howls from the canines of the neighborhood.

"I shoulda gone drinking with the boss," she said. "Another stupid decision by stupid Mari. Can't catch a break."

I wasn't sure if she forgot that not drinking with the boss had been my advice, or if she was letting me off the hook. If it was the latter, I couldn't let that go—I had to take responsibility for my mistake. I placed my hand over hers in what I hoped was a comforting manner. Her skin was dry, her hand cold.

"I can work pro bono for a bit while you get back on your feet—get into the boss's good graces or look for a new job."

I could feel Mari's fingers grip the table. "What does that mean?" she said. "Pro bono?"

I heard a sneeze and retracted my hand, leaning back in my chair to glance toward the bedroom door, which was now slightly ajar. I got up to investigate and Mari followed. Light from the neighbor's kitchen revealed dust particles swirling in the disturbed bedroom air, and I wondered if we'd had a little eavesdropper. Though Lily lay curled up in bed, one leg outside of her blanket, the room lacked the stillness of sleep. She sniffled.

"Think she's getting sick?" I said to Mari.

Mari placed the back of her hand on Lily's forehead. Shook her head, no fever. Lily's eyes were squeezed shut too tightly to be convincing, but I didn't point this out, as the last thing Mari needed was the added worry of Lily having overheard us. Nothing had been said that would make our "arrangement" too obvious, but I doubted that our quick-witted little girl was unaware of something amiss with this supposedly intact family of hers. When she was much younger, she'd thought all fathers only appeared on Thursdays. Now she knew better, of course—and though from time to time (when Mari could afford it) I would sleep on the couch overnight to show up for breakfast Friday morning, she had to know, even if she didn't acknowledge it, that we weren't a typical family. Maybe she worried that we were divorced or estranged, and that we were only pretending for her sake. If she was okay with that— covering her own eyes to keep herself willfully in the dark—then I was okay with it too. Better that she suspect another lie than realize the truth: that even if she uncovered her eyes, she would still be in a pitch-black room.

Mari motioned for us to talk outside, so I followed her down the stairs and out to the stoop. I was surprised by how dark it was. The sun had long set, and the moon had not yet pulled itself above the city edges—or maybe there would be no moon tonight. The sconce by the doorway had gone out, and like with most things in this building, there would be no rush to fix it.

Mari lit a cigarette and picked up where we'd left off.

"So," she said, "this pro thing."

"It means you wouldn't have to pay," I said. "For now. It's not forever; only until you can pay me back."

"Why would you do that?" she said.

It was a fair question. I could tell her that I wanted to take care of them, that being with them made me feel like I was doing good in the world—but that might reek of charity.

"Well," I said, "you're my oldest client." That would make sense—wanting to keep this small but steady stream of revenue. "And I promised you we'd make this work."

"So the promise was . . . a business kinda promise," said Mari.

The cigarette glow lighting Mari's face from below made it difficult to read her expression. The way she licked her teeth—was she disappointed? After all these years of being business partners, did she now want more?

"Mari—"

"I was thinking," said Mari, "that maybe now is the right time to end things, you know, for good."

My chest constricted. I had to fight for a full breath. "Now?" I said, rubbing my sternum, covering up my shortness of breath by clearing my throat. "Why?"

"I'm worried that Lily might like you too much."

Was she using Lily as a cover for her own feelings? I watched the way she flicked cigarette ash and thought I saw a tremble.

"That's okay," I said gently, "isn't it?"

She took a long drag. "I think she likes you more than me."

"Oh."

"We had a fight earlier this week, and I get that she's growing older and it's all normal, but we've never really had fights. Disagreements, sure, but you know Lily has always been so sweet. So easy. But during our argument she said that *Dad* would understand her side of things, which felt worse than if she'd slapped me. And then afterward, when I wanted to apologize, she told me that she needed time to *process* what had happened—as though, as though she were cheese. She's my little girl, and I want her to fly far, sure, but I always want her to come back to me. To me! So what happens if she wants to run to you instead? And then what if I, in a moment of weakness, say something I'll regret? What if I ruin her? Why do I think this way? Am I a terrible person? Am I a bad mom?"

"Never," I said. "You could never be a bad mom, trust me."

"I haven't been picking Lily up from school lately," said Mari.

"I know," I said.

"Don't you want to know why?" said Mari. "Aren't you curious at all about my personal life?"

Of course I was, but for her to ask me felt like a test of my professionalism. And I was a consummate professional. Yet, for some reason, in that moment, I couldn't stop thinking about that cockroach beneath the oven. It was frustrating. No matter how thoroughly you cleaned a house, the pests remained.

"Only if you want to tell me," I said.

Mari sighed, letting the cigarette dangle from her lips. "Consistent, aren't you?" she said. "So damn consistent."

That's who you hired me to be, I wanted to shout. Consistent! A dependable father! So why are you now using those words with such disdain? I could tell Mari wanted more from me, but I needed her to say it: she was still my client, and I could give her whatever she wanted if she would only just say it aloud. Tell me what you want!

Mari shivered, holding herself against the cold. And I, as though pulled by a string of instinct, took two steps forward and wrapped my arms around her, returning the favor she'd given me just weeks before. I continued, calmer now, with what I wanted to say. Yes, please tell me why you've been absent this week, tell me all about your life, and motherhood, and who you are, and who you wish you could have been, and who you can still become, and then I will tell you about myself—about how I wish that I could have been a better son, how I wish I could retract all that hateful vitriol I spewed at my mother, would never have brought the stench of sex into our home, never have left her all alone that evening when she aimed the gun at her heart, emptying a round into the hole that I'd punctured there long before the bullet could. How I wish and wish. But those words remained trapped, caged behind clenched teeth.

"I can be whoever you need me to be," I said, finally, inhaling her citrus and smoke.

Mari peeled away, lit cigarette still in hand. "You're Lily's dad," she said.

"I'm Lily's dad," I repeated in agreement. "But is that enough?"

"Why wouldn't it be?"

Right—why wouldn't it be? "And the pro bono?"

She chewed on the butt of her cigarette. "Okay," she said at last. "Pro bono, for now."

"Thank you," I said, relief loosening my jaw. "Thank you, thank you."

Mari looked sidelong at me as she stamped her cigarette out with the heel of her boot. She opened her mouth as though to say something, but then shut it with a shake of her head.

"Good night," she said, returning into the apartment building, closing the door behind her.

CHAPTER 17

The Rental Stranger app featured banners with attractive, smiling men and women who oozed stock photo happiness. The rentals' profiles would've been similar to dating profiles if the singles promoting themselves also had multiple-personality disorders: CuteGirl777 | Ages: 23–34 | Ethnicity: Indian, South American, Central American, North African, or African-American. Since the holidays were approaching, this narrowed my options considerably. I browsed through the thirty or so profiles that matched my parameters—Fullmoonx was the most highly rated at a respectable 4.1, and I read through her reviews to figure out where the less-than-full marks had come from. Mostly they were complaints about slow responses to messages, which was fine by me as long as it didn't impact her performance. And anyway, the next available option was a 3.8, and I would never rest Lily's future on a 3.8.

Fullmoonx's calendar showed availability for the last Thursday of the month, which meant Lily would have to wait another week to meet her aunt, if the request were accepted. I drafted and redrafted the message—should I divulge that I too was a Rental Stranger? Or would there be less margin for error if she thought that I was the real father? In the end, trusting no one but myself, I went with the latter and sent off the request. Two days later, much to my relief, she accepted.

When I told Lily that she'd have to wait another week to meet her aunt, she was disappointed but only for a second before the excitement of meeting another family member took over, and she bombarded me with questions about a sister I'd never had. Piri (who seemed to be a regular on our walks home now) was confused as to why anyone would be so excited about an aunt, proclaiming that it was cousins who were really the cool ones—older cousins, who snuck you gum and gave you their old video games. When Lily asked if she had any cousins, I had to say no. There were no child rentals on the app. Minors working in theater or film were exempt from child labor laws, but children rentals—well, the theater-of-life argument wasn't going to cut it in court.

Mari wasn't immediately fired, but she remained on shaky ground with her boss, so work was draining her more than usual. The compounded stressors of work, money, and life rendered her capable of only the most perfunctory of interactions with both me and Lily, so I upped my efforts in response, performing a doting husband that Mari accepted without complaint. It seemed like things were back on course, for now. During what little free time I had between assignments, I began to scour job boards for suitable positions for someone of Mari's education and experience, a more sustainable and long-term career path.

Darlene was similarly exhausted from revising her novel, though she also blamed the pouches under her eyes on the oppressive malady of changing seasons combined with the earth's inability to settle on a temperature. Last week it was parka weather and this week, shorts.

"Same characters?" I asked, drinking a can of hard seltzer in Washington Square Park, enjoying the sun warming my face. Our roles were all but forgotten; Darlene had brought a six-pack and said nothing when I accepted a can of pomegranate-hibiscus and checked the label, which said "8 percent ABV."

"Nah," said Darlene. "This one's still about identity and tragedy, but not so on the nose. Trying to hit it with more of a slant. Maybe a short story first to test the waters."

"Does that mean you need me to play someone else, then?"

"Not yet," she said. "You can be yourself for now. Speaking of which, what's your real name, anyway? I can't keep calling you 'brother.'"

I finished my can and Darlene offered me a new one. "Be myself"—now there was a request I'd never heard before. I grinned from behind my can and Darlene rolled her eyes.

"Fine, fine, don't tell me your name," she said. "I get it. Work, confidentiality, blah blah. That's okay. I can just call you Stranger, like"—she half closed her eyes and waggled her fingers toward me as she deepened her voice—"hello, Stranger."

"Was that supposed to be sexy?"

"Was it not?" she said. Then, employing both hands as though she were casting a spell, "You find me sexy, really sexy." She snorted. "Man." Darlene plopped down on the grass, her brown curls spread like a blanket beneath her head. "Writing is hard."

"Why do it, then?" I asked.

"I dunno," she said, staring unblinkingly up at the clear blue sky. "Revenge?"

"Not sure what I expected you to say, but it wasn't that."

"Okay, maybe *revenge* is the wrong word, but"—she screwed her eyes shut—"it's like when you're young, right? And you make up

stories—people are excited and they praise you and say you're creative. But then as you get older, your ability to spin tales is no longer
celebrated; instead we're all told to analyze and deconstruct and
critique and so this, this skill you thought you had is now something
untrustworthy or, worse, childish. But, like, you can't tell me I'm
a good writer when I'm young and then expect me to become an
investment banker when I'm older."

"Isn't revenge a bit childish?" I said, lying down next to her, a
slight buzz from the seltzers settling nicely in my chest.

"Gosh," she said, crossing her forearms over her already closed
eyes, "maybe I am a child. A child stuck on the one thing her parents
told her she was any good at."

"At least your parents think you're good at something."

"They did when I was a kid," she said. "The truth is, I lied to you
about my parents not wanting me to be a writer. It was a stupid lie.
I guess I just wanted that to be the case, you know? That they cared
enough about me to have an opinion about what I chose to do. But
they don't actually care. I could be a drug dealer and they'd still be like,
'That's nice, Darlene, stay safe out there!' You know, they sent me to
boarding school when I was ten years old? How fucked-up is that?"

"Wow," I said, trying to imagine what it would've been like for
me to be separated from my mom at ten, but it was impossible. Who
would have paid for it?

"I know, right?" said Darlene. "And now I'm wasting their money
getting my MFA! So there!"

"No, it's not a waste," I said. "You're good. You're a good writer."

"If only you were an agent or a publisher," said Darlene, "then I'd
take your word for it."

It was true that I'd read none of Darlene's writing, but the alcohol coursing through my bloodstream made me feel oddly generous

with the world and myself. I watched the birds above, beating their wings, and a tender hope blossomed in me like a bruise. Life wasn't easy, but we were all forging ahead, weren't we? Darlene could publish her work and make her parents pay attention to the woman she'd become. I would introduce Lily to her aunt, thereby solidifying my role as a father. I would help Mari find a new job, and when she was better rested, we could talk about the long-term future—about us. We would be happy.

"Just keep going," I said. "We can all do it if we keep going."

After a minute, I turned to face Darlene, but she'd fallen asleep, lips slightly parted, exhausted from the exertions of imagination, as complex and incomprehensible as the tumbling pattern of autumnal leaves. I let her sleep as I watched more birds traverse my field of vision. I raised a hand, trying to capture this feeling of serenity—but the moment I named it as such, it was gone; the shadows of my memories stretched overhead, shading these bright daydreams, reminding me that I didn't deserve such peace, not yet.

CHAPTER 18

On a Thursday afternoon, Lily and I waited by the Sisyphus Stones in Fort Washington Park to meet my sister, her aunt. The stones—precariously balanced atop one another lengthwise, rather than on their flat edges—changed constantly; sometimes there were dozens, and other times none at all. I didn't know who (A bored teen? An artist? An x-treme cairnist?) stacked these creations that looked like people in a procession along the riverfront, but when I first saw them, I wished that I had known about this place a decade ago when I dumped my mother's ashes into the Hudson. Then, at least, there would have been some ceremony—an inanimate audience, who, like her, waited to cross the river Styx. Instead, the only people present had been a few early morning joggers and me—her failure of a son—who, with dry eyes, had emptied the contents of the plastic urn into the gently lapping waves and chucked the container as far as he could into the water, its legacy far outlasting hers.

I had told Fullmoonx to wear a red jacket and to look for the little girl in the yellow coat as we sat on a nearby park bench. Every time a crimson-fitted woman walked or ran by I tried to catch their eye, but none were the fake aunt. After ten minutes, I opened the app and texted, *Are you coming? We are waiting.*

Lily fiddled with the edge of her coat, glancing at me, the river, her hands. When, a few minutes later, I locked eyes with a woman wearing an orange puffer jacket who smiled as she walked closer, Lily grabbed my hand, squeezing my ring and pinky finger.

"Is that her?" said Lily.

Before I could confirm, the woman walked past us—not the rental after all.

"She's always late," I said. "Let's wait a bit longer."

Why were there so many women in red walking by? Was red in this season? I was wearing myself out, swiveling my neck this way and that, my head feeling as though it were attached to a weather-vane. When I was about to give up, Lily spoke again.

"Dad?"

"Yes, Moose?"

Lily's legs dangled off the edge of the bench, the tips of her sneakers barely touching the ground. "What arrangement do you and Mom have?"

"Arrangement? What do you mean?"

"I heard Mom say something about a weird arrangement a while ago."

So Lily had been awake during my conversation with Mari, as I'd suspected. What had she gleaned through the crack in the door? Had she seen how tentative I'd been as I reached my hand out to Mari? How unfamiliar and unfamilial?

"It's my work," I said. "You know, I can't spend much time at home because of it. Even though I want to, of course, see you and your mother."

"It's okay, Dad," she said, looking down at her feet, which knocked together like an anxious heartbeat. "You don't have to lie to me. I'm ten now."

My little Lily, always consoling her parents when she should be the one venting, crying, screaming. Was this the moment she peeped through her fingers to see beyond the insides of palm-pressed eyelids? I could see only two ways forward: either I doubled down on the current act and closed the gap between Lily's fingers, guiding her back into the self-imposed darkness; or I could cover her eyes with my own hands, revising my relationship with Mari toward a divorced-but-friendly storyline. I knew which arc I preferred. Regardless of its flaws, it had worked so far; all I needed was a bit more time and a plan to convince Mari to stay the course indefinitely. For now, I only had to reassure Lily that I wasn't going anywhere. I wrapped an arm around my little girl's shoulders and held her tight to my side.

Lily shuddered, and the girl who'd once told me "Only babies cry" when she fell and skinned her knees (looking disappointed at the pinpricks of blood, as though her body were overreacting) began to weep—her mouth hooking downward as she covered her face with balled fists.

"Oh, hey now," I said, "I think there's been a misunderstanding."

"Are you leaving?" she said.

"Leaving? Of course not!"

"It's Mom's fault, isn't it?"

"No, never! Why would it be?"

"Because she's been—" Lily stumbled. "After work—she's been—"

"It's you!" said a Scandinavian-looking woman walking up to us, balancing a golden-haired toddler on her hip. Although the woman was wearing a maroon windbreaker, a toddler had not been part of the brief. On the app, Fullmoonx had advertised herself as a brunette, and this woman had a head of near-white blond hair. Either this rental was amazing at physical transformations or something unexpected was happening. "Wow!" said the blond woman. "Is this your real daughter?"

This was not Fullmoonx. The way this woman said "Wow!" transported me back three years, when I accompanied her to an abortion clinic as her boyfriend because her real boyfriend had refused to go. When she'd been told at the clinic about the size of her fetus (a kidney bean) she'd exclaimed "Wow!" in the exact same tone. In the end, she'd decided not to go through with the procedure, and now a two-year-old was staring wide-eyed at us and sucking his thumb.

Usually when someone recognized me they had the sense to pretend we'd never met. People who hired Rental Strangers were often assumed to be loners and losers despite the fact that most people who hired me were actually so well-adjusted that they could identify the missing piece in a particular social situation that required the right fit to fill it. But this woman, whose name I couldn't quite place (Astrid or Alice or something like that), was not so discreet.

"Of course this is my daughter," I said, trying not to overstate this and thereby raise the woman's suspicions.

"Wow!" said the woman again, her smile so wide she could swallow Lily whole. She shifted her son to her other hip. "Aren't kids the best?" she said. "I mean, I still can't believe that you'd have a daughter considering your job. Does she know—"

Did this woman have it out for me? Was she projecting her fear that she'd nearly given up the life that now clung to her, and launching a vendetta against me for witnessing her moment of doubt? Or was she simply dumb?

"I'm sorry," I said, "I think you have the wrong person."

"Do I know what?" said Lily, still red-eyed.

"Are you still working as—?" said the woman.

"No," I said, grabbing Lily forcibly by the arm and yanking her out of her seat.

"Ow," said Lily. "That hurts!"

"Hey!" said the woman. "Stop that!"

"She's my daughter!" I said, hot in the face.

Now joggers were stopping and staring; now someone was pulling out a phone. I needed to get out of there, pronto.

But Andrea or Alexa or ArsenicAmyAdeline would not let up, and she crouched down to Lily's eye level, touching her shoulder. "Is this man your father?" she asked, ignoring me completely.

Lily looked at me, looked at the woman with the intense blue stare, looked back at me. I turned away, indicating to Lily that we should leave and also to this busybody of a woman that I wasn't trying to influence Lily's answer in any way. But Lily, already shaken by our earlier unfinished conversation, only became more confused.

"Yeah," she said, with an upward inflection at the end that turned her statement into a question. "I-I think so?"

"You think so?" said the woman, nostrils flaring as though sniffing out prey or preparing for a fight.

"No," said Lily, "he is my dad."

"He's not forcing you—?"

"He's my dad!" said Lily, louder this time, gripping my fingers tightly. I could sense that she understood, now, what was at stake. The two-year-old, thinking he was being yelled at, began to cry.

"Okay, okay," said the woman, standing up and bouncing her little boy. "Just wanted to make sure." She shushed her child, and without a word of apology, turned away on the soles of her New Balance shoes, leaving a confused Lily and her fuming father behind. When I glanced around, the people who'd slowed down to gawk immediately sped up again, realizing that nothing outwardly explosive was happening after all. On the inside, however, it was code red.

"Who was that?" said Lily.

"No idea," I said.

"Why did she say she knew you?"

"Your dad just has one of those faces, you know? Very common, easy to confuse with other people."

"That's not true. You're"—Lily furrowed her brow, looking for the right word— "handsome."

"Thanks," I said.

"Dad?"

"Yeah?"

"You're hurting my hand."

"Oh," I said, and loosened my grip. "I'm sorry, Moose."

At this point, the aunt was a no-show, and we walked back to the apartment so that Lily could do her homework. Lily was silent the entire walk back, which was a relief as it gave me time to sort out my lies. I needed to come up with a compelling and cohesive narrative that tied together what happened with the aunt, where my relationship with Mari stood, and what had happened with that random encounter. I needed time to think, but Lily's silence was also frightening because it meant that she too was developing a narrative in her own mind. I waited for her to bring up anything from this catastrophic afternoon but she didn't say a word. Before Mari returned home, I knew I had to reset the course, so that our fake family life could continue on the straight and narrow and not veer off into brambles of doubt.

"Your aunt just texted to tell me she was called into the hospital suddenly, and that she's really sorry she missed seeing you today."

"Oh," said Lily, not looking up from her homework. "That's okay."

"She says she'll come by next week for sure though!"

Lily looked down at her homework, biting her upper lip as she solved a math problem, perhaps weighing whether to expect her aunt to show up at all. Was it better to subtract x from both sides and therefore not be disappointed? Or should she hold on to hope that the equation might work out, that everything could still fall into place?

"Do you not want to meet her anymore?" I said.

"No!" said Lily. "I do."

"And," I said, "your mom and I are just going through a bit of a rough patch, okay? But we're gonna make it work."

"Mm," said Lily, again not meeting my eye. I could see there was more she wanted to say, but she lowered her head and continued solving her homework.

"What is it?" I asked.

"Nothing," she said, erasing so furiously that she rubbed a hole in the page.

Though I could have pressed more, I realized that for the first time I was afraid of what she might say. I wouldn't pry. She would tell me what was on her mind in due time. That's what I'd bargained for from her mother, after all: time.

I wrote a furious one-star review of Fullmoonx and waited for her to reach out and apologize, or at least try to make things right, but our chat was maddeningly silent as though she had simply disappeared. Delayed responses to messages was one thing, but to not show up at all? A one-star review was not punishment enough. How could she be so unprofessional? Who would I hold accountable for ruining what should have been a great afternoon with Lily? Now, rather than looking back on this day and remembering the warmth of a relative's love, all she would see were more cracks in the family portrait that I'd spent years so delicately painting. Here was a split in the canvas, running between me and Mari, severing her hand from mine. There, a smudge marred my face, so that I looked at Lily and Mari not with love but with unease. No matter how much I covered the canvas with dollops of doting father and brushstrokes of loving husband, in the end, the blemishes prevailed. Damn damn damn. The changes to our arrangement that had been amorphous in my mind would have to become concrete, and soon. I would need to commit more fully to the role of father, show up more days of the week, appease Mari, assuage Lily. Before the end of the year, our family portrait would require something more drastic than another layer of varnish.

But one step at a time. First, I had to find someone trustworthy enough to fill the role of Lily's aunt. That crack, at least, I could seal. I reset my search parameters on the app and scrolled through the short list of available rentals one more time. What else could I do? My contacts list was empty.

CHAPTER 19

'll do it," said Darlene, pressing so far forward that the glass of IPA in front of her teetered. "I can be the aunt."

"That's insane," I said, shifting her drink to the side. "I can't have one client working for another." Half the sidewalk was occupied by our table, pushed up against the outside walls of a pub. Sticking a leg out would have taken down at least three people shuffling home from work, heads buried in their phones, unfeeling as a progression of ants.

I was still on edge about everything that had happened at the park and Darlene, perceptive as a writer should be, had noticed. When she asked, "What's eating you?" I couldn't come up with a convincing enough lie—in part because there was no backstory for me to pull from. Although I still wore his hair, clothes, and glasses, I was no longer acting as Serge. It would be unprofessional to suddenly change my looks even though I wasn't even entirely sure what service Darlene was paying for anymore. This would need to be remedied, but later. I had other—bigger—issues for now.

"I'm a good actress," said Darlene. "You said so yourself."

"When you're playing a character you wrote," I said, scratching at my arm. I'd developed a rash in the nook of my elbow from stress.

"We already have experience being brother and sister."

"I guess that's true."

"So?"

I stopped scratching, afraid it might bleed, scab, and scar, marking me in a permanent way. "Why would you want to do it?" I asked.

"We're friends," she said with a shrug, as though this were something we both knew to be true. As though I'd had friends throughout my adult life. Was this what friendship was about after high school? Someone who noticed your troubles and cared about you, at no cost? How tiring it must be, to do so much for so little in return. In school, friendship was an incidental by-product of liking the same movies or being good at kicking a ball on a grassy field. Rarely did we take care of one another; most of the time we competed and tried to claim what was ours, but we still stuck together because we didn't want to be alone. But now, as adults, people *chose* friendship—this fickle arrangement that could be taken away at any time without recourse—but why? To not be lonely? There was nothing wrong with being alone, at least that's what my mother always said—"I'm alone now, aren't I?" she'd say to me. "It's better this way. Other people become too obsessed with you, jealous of your successes, high off your failure."

But Darlene was different: she wasn't asking for anything. She was offering to help. And for a moment I considered it, before remembering that this was a job for a professional. "I'm already searching on the app," I said. "But thanks, I appreciate it."

"Pooh," said Darlene.

That evening, still with no leads on a potential aunt, I attended a Halloween party upstate with an older man who wanted to relive his youth while his wife was out of town. "You want me to wing-man?" I asked.

"No," he said, "I just want to let loose. Here's some Narcan just in case."

The party, spread out over the many floors and lawns of a mansion, was an over-the-top extravaganza of Burning Man as envisioned by Jay Gatsby. At the entrance, crystal chandeliers shone not from the ceiling but were strewn across the floor so that partygoers had to circumvent these iridescent centerpieces. Large porcelain vases lined the hallways, graffitied in gold. Caviar was served on Ritz crackers and accompanied with cocktail napkins made of silk, tossed after a single use. My client was already flying high, bumping into expensive-looking antique furniture and running through decorative leaf litter that brought the outdoors inside. If Halloween was about scary, I supposed this was frightening in its own way, the trashed decadence of an overfattened empire poised for its inevitable fall.

In a greenhouse, fanned ferns, bulbous succulents, and potted citrus trees crowded around a teepee of white stretch fabric, inside which a dozen or so people sat. A woman in a red dress with loose sleeves and a golden matha patti atop her white wig (the lace front didn't match her skin tone, an amateur move) lifted her arms.

"Come," she said, "the tea ceremony is about to begin."

"Ohhhh shit," said my client, wobbling toward the tent, "I love ceremonies." He plunked down onto a throw pillow, and I sat next to him on the floor, the marble cool beneath my palms. A small butane fire in the middle of the teepee heated an ornate copper teakettle.

"This tea, weary travelers," said the woman, lowering her voice for dramatic effect, "will soothe your heart and soul if you let it. Now"—she lifted the kettle with a flourish, as a young man with pointed ears, like an elf straight out of Rivendell, passed out pounded copper cups with steaming tea in them—"the first sip is bitter." She demonstrated by drinking directly from the spout of the kettle, steaming tea hitting her tongue without so much as a flinch.

"Excuse me," I whispered to the budget Legolas. "Are there drugs in here?" Per rule two, I would not partake in anything that the DEA could come after me for.

"It's medicine," he said.

I sniffed at my cup.

"Rooibos and betel nut," he hissed before turning away.

I took a sip that tasted medicinal and metallic, and swallowed. "Healing is a process that can often be unpleasant, but if we acknowledge and allow it to happen, then the second sip"—another pour from the kettle—"and the third and the fourth"—how she hadn't first-degree burned her mouth was beyond me—"will be better. And before we know it, we have allowed for the process of healing to take over—we can let go of a lifetime of hardship, of chewing on and obsessing over life's bitter and harsh edges." I wondered if she were rentable on the app; she'd fit the bill for an unwell aunt, if the illness were grandiosity. It seemed that I was the only naysayer, however, as everyone around me slowly sipped their tea and marveled at the way their palates could acclimate to bitterness. I put my cup on the floor, not taking another sip. If acclimation was healing, then I didn't want to heal. To heal was to forget, and I couldn't—wouldn't—forget. For in every dark room I saw my mother's ruined body waiting in the shadows: accusatory, demanding repentance. And I was repenting. Hundreds of clients later, did their happiness outweigh her misery? Not yet, but I had the sense that if I could commit fully to someone else's happiness—not just for a day or a few weeks, but for a lifetime—to do for Mari and Lily what I couldn't do for my own mother—then maybe I could be forgiven. Maybe I would no longer be afraid of the dark.

On the other side of me, a young woman in a gold lamé bra and tutu made of what looked like Brillo pads knocked my cup over, spilling the amber liquid onto the floor and into the seat of my pants.

"Whoopsie," she said, eyes not quite focusing on anything. She leaned into me and whispered, "I'm really high."

In the restroom, inconveniently located in an annex outside the main mansion as though the realities of piss and shit were best kept as far away as possible, I finally had a moment of quiet beyond the reach of the electronic music and my client's incessant chatter. In the mirror, I checked to make sure there were no flaws in my getup: I was a thirty-four-year-old man of means, spending the evening with his slightly older friend. I was accustomed to such lavish parties and didn't consider trivialities such as how much the electricity bill might cost to light up this fifty-room mansion. I smoothed out the cynical wrinkles around my mouth and put on a pleasant, nothing-behind-the-eyes expression.

I took a moment to check my phone for any responses to my queries (or an apology from Fullmoonx) and, to my surprise, found a message from Ajay. It was a request for a second meeting, sent at one thirty in the morning. He was clearly drunk, writing to me as his *buddy* with whom he wanted to *crush puss* again, saying that we had a *great night lats time dindt we?* It was so depressing that I deleted it immediately. Ajay, for all his bluster, had no friends to reach out to except a man he'd once hired for an evening and then proceeded to trash online. I almost felt sorry for him—but the wealthy didn't pay for my pity.

Plenty of people had tried to be buddy-buddy with me over

the years—thinking they might get a discount, or learn the tricks of the trade, or what have you. And though Ajay's solicitation was the most egregious, it was nothing new. Standing in front of the dimly lit bathroom mirror, I finally understood why I had considered accepting Darlene's offer to play Lily's aunt. When she called me her friend, it wasn't the first time a client wanted to be friends, but it was the first time I'd felt the desire to reciprocate.

Back in the mansion, I found my client falling ass first into a claw-foot bathtub full of strawberries as a woman singing an aria dressed in full tulle dumped champagne on his head.

CHAPTER 20

I spent all my free time searching for a replacement for Fullmoonx, but no one good was free on such short notice, and Lily's faith (along with my standing as a reliable parent) couldn't take another no-show.

"Let me guess," said Darlene, cross-legged on the sticky couch of an Alphabet City dive, "my niece still needs an aunt."

I fished a fruit fly out of my whiskey sour with my pinky.

"I'm telling you," she said, "I can do it."

Four college students bounced around on the waterbed in the corner, laughing and sloshing their drinks down each other's sides.

"Okay," I relented. It was an unprecedented move for me, allowing two clients to meet, but I was out of time and options. "Okay, okay, okay. Okay."

Darlene laughed. "But tell me, is it okay?"

"Don't test me."

"Oui, boss."

I set my drink down and Darlene followed suit. "There's a lot to prepare in a very short amount of time," I said. "For example, where did we grow up? What were our parents like? What did we like to do as kids, teens, young adults, now? Why are you here? What do you do here? Why are you going to California? What do you want?"

"Sounds like creating a fictional character," Darlene said, picking up her drink again and taking a big gulp.

"Sure, but you have to bring that character to life such that you know how they'll respond to any situation, because unlike fiction, you don't control what the other characters say or do. And you can't delete. Or start over."

"Don't worry," said Darlene. "I did improv in college."

"Shouldn't you be working on your novel?"

"Who are you, my thesis advisor?" she said, ringing the edge of her cup with her middle finger. "It's no longer a novel, remember? Short stories, because I hear that's harder to sell and I'm a masochist who hates money. Also, I decided to add another semester."

"Your program is okay with that?"

"Why wouldn't they be?" said Darlene. "More moolah for them."

Despite what she said about her parents, and how she dressed like a cousin of the crust punks loitering on St. Mark's with their three-legged dog, at least Darlene's mother and father made sure she never wanted for anything. Anyone who could afford extra semesters of a writing program had money (some of which, I had to remind myself, went into my pockets).

"So when do I finally get to meet the little girl?" said Darlene.

"Thursday," I said.

"As in, two days from now?"

"Yes."

"Shit."

With that, we got to work outlining Darlene's character: the long-term illness that had kept her away from her niece for so long, the doctors in New York who were finally able to help her live a near-normal life, and the memoir she was working on about her struggles ("I don't know how to talk convincingly about anything besides writing," said Darlene almost apologetically).

On Wednesday, after a rushed date with a college student who wanted to show off her mature boyfriend to her a cappella group, Darlene and I met up to run through scenarios one last time.

"Why didn't you show up last week?" I said, tilting my head and pitching my voice up to mimic a little girl's.

"I got called in by the doctor."

"For what?"

"He wanted to go over a test result."

"Are you okay?" I sucked on a fistful of hair.

Darlene snorted and then, realizing that she'd broken character, cleared her throat. "Sorry, sorry—I won't laugh if she does that, but you look ridiculous. Yeah, um, I'm fine. It was a false alarm. Do you think she knows what a false alarm is?"

I nodded. My wig tasted like plastic and burnt coffee. I pulled the strands out of my mouth. "She's a smart kid."

"How smart?"

"Very."

"And she still thinks you're her real dad?"

I frowned.

"Sorry," said Darlene. "Off script."

I cleared my throat, no longer pretending to be Lily. "So when she asks you about visiting again?"

"I'll tell her that I have to go back to California to take care of my cats."

"What are your cats' names?"

"Uh, Mimi and Tequila."

"Tequila?"

"Sorry, it was right in front of me. Use what you got, you know?"

"Sure."

"But I'll write."

"All right what?"

"I will write, as in, I have to leave town but I'll send her emails from time to time. Stay in touch."

"Hmm," I said.

"I don't really have to send her anything. Or you can write them for me if you want," said Darlene. "It'll be better than cutting her off from her aunt completely."

It wasn't a bad idea, and I thanked Darlene for her time. We'd practiced to the point where I was confident Darlene could last a few hours and convince Lily that we were related (though from a previous marriage, if Lily asked why Darlene and I didn't look very much alike—more branches to add to the family tree).

We were scheduled to meet at the zoo on Thursday afternoon, where I hoped that Lily might be distracted enough by animals to not cross-examine Aunt Darlene. I was determined to give Lily a perfect afternoon that she could keep in her pocket like a well-polished marble, reminding her of all the good times in case of tempestuous days ahead.

CHAPTER 21

Fall was nearing its end, and the wilting leaves in their umbers and ambers lifted their heads up to the sun one last time before giving in to the wind's demands, spiraling down to their final resting place beneath our feet. Darlene was already waiting for us at the entrance to the zoo. When she spotted me, she began to wave eagerly in our direction. Lily, who much to my surprise was wearing the blue coat over her favorite pastel-pink romper with the shoulder ties that wouldn't hold, took a step back, hiding behind me while we were still twenty paces away. The little girl who, minutes earlier, had been eagerly chatting away about the myriad things she would ask her aunt had become shy in an instant.

"I wish Piri was here," she said. We'd left him at the school gates; he'd watched us leave with a dejected smile. "He's funnier than me."

"You don't have to be funny," I said. "Just be yourself."

"But what if—"

"Don't worry," I said. "She's family."

"Lily!" said Darlene, coming up and giving her niece a hug. Darlene was wearing a cardigan over a buttoned-up blouse tucked into blue jeans. I was surprised that she owned such a basic, matronly outfit, though upon closer inspection I gathered that the cardigan was new, from its department store scent and the *s s s s* strip that I surreptitiously peeled off her back. "How are you?" Darlene asked Lily.

"Good," said Lily, reaching for my fingers.

"Any animals you really wanna see today?"

"Um," said Lily, watching a squirrel scamper up a nearby tree.

"The penguins?" I prompted her.

"Oh yeah," she said. "Right."

Lily conversed easily with adults—almost more easily than with other kids—but she struggled to string together more than two words in front of her aunt. Secretly, I was relieved. The more shy Lily was during this outing, the less chance of a slipup from Darlene.

"Nice hair," said Darlene as I flashed my tickets to the agent at the entrance. She'd never seen me outside of the grunge outfit with the black wig.

"Thanks," I said. "Just got it cut."

I gave her a warning look and she grinned cheekily.

"I'm on my best behavior today, dearest Brother," she said, breezing by me and then turning back to mouth, "this is fun."

Inside, we passed the sea lion pool, where the sleek bronze mammals propelled themselves out of the water and onto the rocks, their smell reminding me of the subway entrances in Times Square.

"Oh shit," said Darlene. "It stinks."

I cleared my throat.

"Whoops, I mean—"

"That's okay," said Lily. "You can swear."

"You're a cool kid, arencha?" said Darlene.

Lily smiled and fiddled with her jacket's fur trim. She'd been called clever, articulate, hardworking, and mature. But never cool. It hadn't occurred to me how much Lily might've craved that compliment.

At the penguin enclosure, Lily took her aunt's hand as I trailed behind, which was fine by me. I didn't care for birds. In one of my earliest memories (so distant now that it feels like myth), a flock of pigeons swooped toward me as I ran, screaming, to hide behind my mother. But more so than my own fear, I remember my mother's disappointment in me: from the lock of her knees to the way she gripped my narrow shoulders as she pulled me out from behind her, as if she could broaden them with the force of her palms. Perhaps she had a premonition that a boy who couldn't protect himself from pigeons would do nothing to protect her. Or perhaps the story is colored by my own embarrassment. It's hard to remember clearly now. After nearly a decade since her passing, she was becoming less of a person and more of a face behind a window—a smeared pane that I avoided gazing through, though I caught accidental glimpses from time to time of a face shrouded in shadow and shame.

Lily was warming up to her aunt, rattling off penguin facts like, did you know that emperor penguins could leap six feet out of the water and little penguins, as their names might indicate, are the smallest species of penguins? Darlene nodded along, saying things like, "No shit?" and "Where'd you learn that?" Though I enjoyed Lily sharing her font of knowledge, it had always struck me as odd the way we memorized facts in school and called it an education: our schooling having us falsely believe that facts could serve us once we graduated into the real world—as though anyone could even agree upon one statement as fact anymore, as though there were such a thing as truth. Tell me the sky is blue and the ancient Greeks will beg to differ.

I'd guessed Darlene wouldn't be good with kids and she wasn't—
saying exactly what was on her mind in language either too florid or
vulgar for young ears—but she was good for Lily, who never liked
being talked down to anyway. And this was how we visited the
animals: Darlene and Lily hand in hand, me trailing behind. Every
so often Lily would glance back to make sure I was still there, and
my heart squeezed.

Having seen most of the cages and enclosures, we finally sat
down to unwrap and eat some Cornettos that Darlene bought. Unlike when Lily and I sat alone on a park bench, the addition of Darlene meant that no one gave us a second glance; her womanhood
indicated to the New York public that this situation was peaceful,
normal. Somehow, we were more of a family with the addition of
one female stranger than we had been without—a feminine power.

Lily carefully peeled the paper around her ice cream in a spiral
as Darlene ripped into hers, the paper falling in swirls around her
feet like a galaxy.

"When are you going back to California?" said Lily.

"Soon," said Darlene.

"I wish you could stay longer," said Lily, which was about the
most I'd ever heard her ask of anyone.

"Me too," said Darlene. "Hey, why don't I get your email address
and we can keep in touch?"

Lily happily dictated her school email to Darlene, who wrote it
in her phone.

"I'll email you," said Darlene.

"Can I read part of your book?" said Lily.

"It's a bit dark," said Darlene.

"I read at a high school level," said Lily. "I read *Of Mice and Men*
recently."

"Well, sure then," said Darlene. "I don't see why not."

I added ghostwriting a chapter of a nonexistent memoir to my to-do list.

"I love the zoo," said Lily.

"A slightly depressing yet surprisingly captivating delight," said Darlene.

"I'm so glad you two finally got to meet," I said. Darlene had done well for her first and only assignment. She'd been a bit too focused on the Lily angle and hadn't really played up the sibling relationship between us—but Lily hadn't noticed, fixated as she was on her cool aunt from California (who nonetheless let slip New Yorkisms like "wait on line" instead of "wait in line").

As Lily walked off to toss her wrapper, Darlene leaned back into the bench, one arm draped over the back. "Good kid," she said.

"Sure is."

"So when are you gonna tell her?"

"Tell her what?"

"That you're not her real dad."

I watched as Lily stopped to admire some pigeons by the trash can, their necks shimmering like heat waves.

"That's up to her mother to decide."

"Don't you think it's better to do it sooner rather than later?"

"It's not my decision to make," I said again.

"Do you love her?"

"Excuse me?"

"Do you love her, like, do you care about her outside of the job?"

Lily was on her way back now, walking with her toes slightly pointed inward. I could already tell that she would grow to be taller than her mother, able to see beyond the limited horizons that penned in Mari's world. I hoped she'd outgrow my world too.

But in order to facilitate her growth, I had to stay, stand guard, do my job.

"It's work," I said. "I care when I'm paid to care."

"That's cold, man," said Darlene with a whistle. "I've known the girl for a few hours and I already love her."

"Sure," I said, with a chuckle, "as if love were that easy."

When Lily returned, Darlene asked her, "Do you know what love is?"

And Lily, taken aback, looked between me and her aunt, suddenly nervous as though this were a graded quiz. "Um," she said. "A feeling?"

"Sure is, kiddo," said Darlene, "a good feeling, too. Everyone should feel it—isn't that right, Brother?"

I frowned. "Sure." And then, weary of where Darlene was taking this line of inquiry, I stood up. "Your aunt's tired. I think we should let her get back and rest."

"Sorry," Darlene said, blowing a strand of hair off her face. "I guess it's too touchy-feely of a subject for your old man." She bent down for a hug. "I love you!" she said as she wrapped her arms around the little girl.

Lily, who was accustomed to acts but not words of love, was so shocked by this easy declaration that the light caught in the corner of her eye glistened. After a moment she whispered, "I love you too," into Darlene's tangled mass of hair, a sentiment so private that I turned my face away, afraid to look at such vulnerability head-on.

CHAPTER 22

Over dinner, Lily spoke of Darlene nonstop. Mari, who'd returned from a particularly grueling day at work, nodded along, two nods away from nodding off into her lasagna. Before turning in for the night, Lily hesitated at the bedroom door.

"What's wrong?" I asked.

"Nothing," she said, looking between her mother, who was rotely checking receipts, and me, wiping down the countertops—in other words, an average evening. Mari was balancing cash inflow with outflow, trying to stanch the bleed, not registering Lily's presence. So I was the only one who saw the earnest trepidation on Lily's face— that desire to express in words what words could not hold. "Um," said Lily, still hanging in the doorway. "I love you."

But Mari merely nodded, not hearing her daughter's voice over the roar of anxiety in her head as she tried to make the numbers on her phone calculator tie out. If Mari couldn't respond, then I could. All I had to say was "I love you too"—then maybe my words would lift Mari's anxiety-induced blinders, and she would see that her little girl was testing the waters of expressing affection, and maybe this would convince Mari that our experimental family was working out after all. It was easy. Four words. I'd said it to countless other people in my long career. And yet, Darlene's question, "Do you love her?" rang in my ear. Did I love her? Did *I* love her? Would I stab my mother and leave her to the shark to let Lily get away?

"Sweet dreams, Moose," I said.

Lily's face closed itself off, followed shortly by the door.

Once I returned to my apartment, I spent the evening composing an email to Lily from her aunt and even signed off with a *Love you*, but then stared at the draft for an hour, unable to hit send. I resisted the urge to scratch at my slowly healing rash. What was the point if I couldn't tell her directly? Of course the character of Lily's father loved his daughter—wasn't that enough? Wasn't the staid performance of love and care everything anyone really wanted? Did deeper feeling have to exist for the act to have meaning? Because what about those parents, like Mari, whose lives were given meaning simply by their child's presence, and yet could never say that out loud? But it was clear, wasn't it? When parents loved their child: when they subconsciously walked first into new spaces to scope out potential danger, or gave their kid the best slices of the apple, gnawing on the core for themselves, or when they handed their child a cup of water before the child even realized he was thirsty? I did those things for Lily, but only when I was paid to. I would do the same for any other child indiscriminately if their parents were my clients.

I deleted the email and shut my laptop. Lily could wait a few days to hear from her aunt; for now, rest.

CHAPTER 23

My phone mimicked birdsong and chimes to inform me it was eight in the morning, and the cars on Canal blasted their horns to let me know it was time to wake the fuck up. I'd drafted and redrafted my email until four in the morning before giving up, and was thoroughly exhausted. Through sheer force of will, I began my morning routine—starting with my fixation on the overhead light fixture—but my body was limp with fatigue, and my eyes could hardly focus, so after a few minutes I gave up, my right hand cramping. Only when the coffee hit my veins did I feel I might be okay for today's performances.

I needed to meet two clients today before heading up to a Friday afternoon wedding in Connecticut, and by the time I dragged myself back in front of the bathroom mirror (contouring my face to accentuate my Caucasian features, bringing the brow bone forward and lifting the nose), the blue bags beneath my eyes required a heavy amount of concealer to mask. With only minutes to spare, I donned a tux, polished my shoes, and rushed out of my apartment. Once safely on the train, I slid into an empty seat next to a hunched-over middle-aged man scarfing down a slice of pepperoni pizza like he was sinning and had to finish it in the time it took God to blink. Maybe it was treif, but I wanted to tell him to slow down so I wouldn't have to resuscitate a choking man. In any case, I was pretty sure that God didn't care what happened on Metro-North.

After the pizza vacuum wiped his lips on his sleeve and fell into an open-mouthed slumber, I picked up where I'd left off on my best man speech. When the client first wrote me about how he and his future wife were getting into role-playing, I'd wondered why they wanted me to include this very private detail into the speech—but then he'd continued, describing how they played with a group of six people, and that he was a cleric. Normally I'd have a best man speech locked and loaded at least a day in advance, but other pre-occupations had been top of mind as of late. On the train, I edited my standard speech to include a few Dungeons and Dragons references, but ended up getting lost in the monster list—mind flayers, owlbears, trolls. I wondered if Lily might be into this kind of thing. She hadn't gone through a high fantasy phase yet, and she clearly liked animals. I allowed myself to finally feel relief that the day at the zoo had gone well. The aunt snafu was over. Happiness. One step at a time.

I jolted awake when the pizza gobbler nudged my shoulder. "Excuse me," he said. "This is my stop."

I glanced at the sign outside and realized that this was my stop too—that I'd fallen asleep while reading the list, somewhere between unicorn and vampire. I patted my pockets frantically to make sure I still had my wallet and keys before darting out of the train car.

Out in the Connecticut suburbs, there were no proper sidewalks, and I skirted lawns and flower beds while avoiding oncoming traffic. The sun shone high overhead on a cloudless day, so as a black car pulled up next to me, I had to shield my eyes to see who was inside as the window rolled down slowly.

"Need a ride?" said a man in a British accent. I squinted and recognized that it was none other than the old man from the cemetery who'd asked if I had any questions for him—this time, however, presenting as a spry older gentleman with his white hair gelled back and sporting a pair of tortoiseshell glasses.

Despite the dropping temperatures, I could feel heat collecting in my neck and lower back. The venue was about a mile away, and it wouldn't do to show up steeped in sour sweat.

"Sure," I said, with a similar accent, beginning my assignment a touch early. And then, once in the air-conditioned car, "Thanks. Are you heading to the Marriott?"

"Indeed I am," said the old man.

"I'm guessing as part of the wedding party?"

"Father of the groom," said the old man, lightly touching his chest as though proud of his son's accomplishment.

I laughed and the old man, quick on the uptake, laughed as well.

"Let me guess," he said. "You're my other son."

"Good to see you again, Dad," I said.

"Good to see you again too, son," said the old man.

Without anyone to perform for, we drove the rest of the way in silence, though I watched the way he tapped on the steering wheel in time with a song playing in his head. I was sure he watched me too as I checked my makeup in the side mirror, wiping away the dried trail of drool from when I'd fallen asleep on the train.

The groom was delighted that his father and brother had appeared together at the same time, making a good show of what a close-knit family we were to his bride, who had no idea this was a charade.

"It's so good to finally meet your family," she said, coming out of her suite to say hi, sprouting wayward pins from her hair. "You must be exhausted from your flight!"

"A bit knackered," I replied, "but happy to meet you at last!"

"Yes, good to make your acquaintance, love," said the old man.

The bride and groom didn't seem to notice this discrepancy between the old man's and my slightly different regional accents. But the bride, after hearing both of us talk, did smack her future husband's arm playfully and ask, "Why don't you have a sexy British accent?" The groom's face pinched a bit at this obvious oversight. "He summered in the States," said the old man, without missing a beat. "Became American right quick."

By the time the reception started, I desperately needed more coffee; the exhaustion was starting to make me feel like I was floating an inch off the ground. I was entering a giddy state of tiredness. The white floral arrangements at the center of each table became pillows where I could rest my head, and the tablecloth a blanket to tuck into—though, of course, I would not. I only had to hold out through my speech, and then I could coast by for the rest of the evening, perhaps even leave early. Normally I would have memorized my best man's speech, but I'd barely had time to finish writing, much less memorize this one. When the MC handed me the mic, I pulled up the note on my phone and, to my horror, found that while dozing off I'd mostly written fragments of sentences ("every day a natural 20"), which I now had to make sense of on the spot. "Wow," I said into the mic partway through, "this jet lag is bloody brutal!"—to which a few people chuckled. I looked to the groom, worried that my performance was lacking and he would be seething—but he was too absorbed by his bride, who was beaming with happiness now that both sides of the family had bridged the Atlantic, to be together at last.

"Good speech," said the old man as I sat back down at the family table.

"Yours was better," I said truthfully.

"Your old man still has a few tricks up his sleeves," he said, patting me on the shoulder. "Can't let you catch up too quickly."

"Cheers to that," said the bride's father. Everyone at the table laughed, and the bride's brother sitting next to me snorted, giving me a glance like we shared an inside joke about sons and dads. I winked back.

"Cheers," I said, and the table toasted once again to the union of our families.

Now that the speeches were over, along with my five minutes in the spotlight, I could relax. I had planned on sitting and maybe making polite conversation with other guests for the rest of the night, before one of the bridesmaids dragged me onto the dance floor, where the music told us to get low. As she crouched down, she lost her balance and reached for my thighs for support.

"Whoops," she said, as I helped her up. She placed a hand on my chest and lurched forward a bit, as though her center of gravity were two steps ahead.

"Need some water?" I asked, gently holding her steady by the shoulders. She and I had conversed some throughout the afternoon about the weather, and her work as a legal assistant, and why it was such a bummer my flight was delayed and I couldn't make it to the morning rehearsal (the real reason being that the groom didn't want to shell out any more than necessary for my services; he was a penny-pincher—who else had Friday weddings?). From the way her friends kept sneaking looks in our direction, I could tell that she'd been talking to them about me.

"Omigosh," she said, "say *water* again."

I left her to go to the bar and found the old man leaning against the counter, drinking whiskey on the rocks. "Why don't you go for it?" he said. Clearly he'd noticed the way she'd been watching me the entire wedding, had seen her fall into my arms.

"You know I can't," I said, absentmindedly scratching the inner crook of my elbow. "Gets messy if they ask about me."

"You're gonna be a whole continent away tomorrow," he said. "She knows what she's doing and it's just for a good time. I would have, when I was younger."

"Really?"

"Sure. Got me in trouble a few times, but worth it. Enjoy your youth while you can."

We both looked out over the dance floor, and I tried to see it as he saw it—a playground that he'd outgrown but still remembered fondly. I wondered if he had a real family now, or if he was too old for lust, or if he thought it wouldn't do for the father of the groom to hook up at his own son's wedding. A father hoping for his son to enjoy the same experiences he'd also had—was this how fathers and sons interacted? One life slowly taught to mimic the other until an earnest replica had been made, and the original (in itself also a replica of its father) eventually wasting away? Did fathers and daughters work the same way? Mothers and sons?

My fake father ordered me a whiskey neat and then pushed me back out into the fray, to enjoy life's carnal pleasures in his stead. I could see it all more clearly: sweat-speckled chests and the wine-rouged cheeks, flirtation thick in the air. Unless clients explicitly stated that they wanted me on the dance floor, I usually avoided the crush of bodies gyrating to "Crazy in Love." But tonight I felt lighter, like things were moving in the right direction. Maybe, just maybe, I could have sex tonight—intertwine our limbs without thinking of the void, wake up in the morning and not be alone. She wasn't a client; I wasn't breaking any rules. I located the bridesmaid from earlier and handed her a glass of water, which she drank greedily. Her lipstick had smudged a bit across her cheek. I wiped at it with the pad of my thumb. She kissed my palm. Since I hadn't relieved myself that morning, my body moved against my will and an urgent need pressed into my slacks.

"Come upstairs for a bit," she whispered, cupping her hand behind my ear. "Should be empty."

I was too lightheaded to say no.

Taking my hand, she led me to the elevator and up to the fourth floor, where we entered what appeared to be the bridesmaids' suite. Makeup, empty glasses of champagne, bath towels, hair curlers, and clothes hangers littered the room. She swept a pair of jeans off the bed and plopped down. Walking toward her, I thought of the old man, and in that moment I felt like his puppet—the strings tugging my feet up and down, moving for his sake. As she unzipped my pants, I saw the thin lines of my mother's lips while reading yet another script about love and sex. The bridesmaid pulled me down for a kiss, her gin-soaked tongue rough against mine.

"Hmm," she said, touching the outside of my boxers. The pressing desire was subsiding, and I tried to push thoughts of my mother far, far away. Instead, I concentrated on the bridesmaid's slender shoulders, freckled skin, her blond hair spread out like a wispy mane. As her hand slipped beneath my waistband and I felt her cool grip, I imagined that it was my own hand, so as not to risk being consumed by the fear of losing control. After a few minutes she said, "What's wrong?" and I, not wanting her to see the look on my face, flipped her around and began unzipping her dress. The act of peeling her slick dress from her soft body, like the membraned shell off a soft-boiled egg, was arousing. It was a pleasant surprise to see a mole here, a dimple there. I kissed the small of her back.

"Hold on," she said, turning back around and covering her chest with her arms (though there wasn't much to hide). She quickly shuffled to the door and shut off all the lights. The room, with its blackout curtains drawn, was thrown into pitch darkness.

I felt as though I'd gone blind.

Biting back a scream, I hurtled toward the sliver of light beneath the door, knocking into ironing boards and suitcases as I pulled up my pants. I fumbled with the door handle and then rushed into the hallway, the naked bridesmaid shrieking as I bolted past her.

"What's wrong?" she cried after me. I was already five paces away, ten. "It's the mole, isn't it?" Fifteen, twenty. "I'm getting it removed soon!"

I felt faint. Back downstairs, the wedding had already dispersed as uniformed workers stacked chairs and gathered floral arrangements; the revelers had moved on to an after-party and my father, the old man, was nowhere to be seen. This was for the best. I didn't want to tell him that I'd failed in the task he'd set out for me. I left the venue and began sprinting the mile back to the train station. My head pounded. I kept pumping my legs until they felt like my own again, without strings, without a puppeteer. My lungs screamed. I let them scream. I arrived just as the last train to New York City pulled into the station, and once I slunk into the plasticky seat in a nearly empty and well-lit train, I immediately fell into a deep sleep, awakened only when the train conductor shook my shoulder and told me we were at Grand Central and that I'd better not be dead.

With the last of my battery life, I checked the app to see if the groom had any complaints. A full payment and five stars, though only a 15 percent tip. I supposed that meant it had been a good day, but I felt like I had chugged a bottle of Hennessy and then run a marathon—my mouth was bone-dry and my body ached. I'd come close to sleeping with someone for the first time in a decade, but the doom was there, even if it had been momentarily obscured by the twin fogs of exhaustion and alcohol. Perhaps it was enough to know I could still have sex if I wanted to. My abstinence was by choice. It wasn't physiological; it was intentional—this seemed an important distinction as the latter felt more like proper penance.

Back in my apartment the light was on as always, and I didn't bother changing out of my tux. I plugged my phone in, lay on top of my sheets, and closed my eyes, another successful job done.

CHAPTER 24

In Terminal B, the glass panes were poor insulation against the frost of the bomb cyclone that touched down in New York seemingly overnight.

"Seventy last week and five below this, can you believe it?" said the man in front of me in line. "It's the end-times, I tell ya." He spoke the way most people over the age of fifty do—to the general public—like everyone needed your opinion, likely because no one cared about that opinion at home. Behind me, a young woman shuffling a mewling kitten in a pink cat carrier looked, by the grease in her hair and the glint in her eye, on the brink of a meltdown.

"Can I say hi to your cat?" I said.

"I'm so sorry," she said, hoisting the shoulder strap of the carrier up. "It's our first time flying and he won't stop meowing; I think he's nervous."

"Cats can sense their owners' stress," I said, waggling a finger in front of the tabby doing barrel rolls in an effort to escape its cloth-and-mesh prison.

"Oh God," she said.

"Don't worry," I said. "Everything will be fine. Where are you heading?"

"I'm trying to get to Austin," she said. "Where the weather is always seventy degrees and there's squirrels instead of rats. Why did I come all the way to the East Coast to get a kitten? What was I thinking?" Her hoodie and sweatpants were far too thin for the winter weather outside.

The cat yowled plaintively.

"You'll be fine," I said. And then, a bit louder, "I've been flying with this airline since I was in college and it's never let me down. You'll get to where you need to go."

She craned her neck to scan the dozens of people in line ahead of her and noted the snake of almost fifty people behind.

I shifted my suitcase to my other hand. "I'm still waiting for my wife so why don't you take my spot in line. I should probably move toward the back since she'll be a while."

"Thank you," the harried young woman said without hesitation.

"I'm not in a rush either," said the middle-aged man in front of me. "Go ahead."

"Wow," said the young woman. "Um, happy holidays."

At the back of the line, the stench of anxiety was more pungent. A family of four—with one child in a stroller and the other bouncing around like a pinball—looked particularly on the brink of panic.

"Excuse me," I said. "I think families with young children can check in at bag drop."

The father, bald with a reddish-brown mustache, frowned, but his wife, who was holding on to the toddler by the neckline of his sweater, thanked me. I assured them both that if I was wrong (I wouldn't be; I had just received a briefing on the airline's policies that morning), they could return to their place in the line in front of me, no problem.

"I fly this airline a lot," I assured the people around me. "They're really reasonable."

"Right?" said a woman who I recognized as the other rental they'd hired to do this job with me. "I've been flying them since college and this kind of thing has never happened before!"

The two of us struck up a conversation about the merits of our employer, a skit we repeated at least five more times throughout the rest of the day. At the end of our long shift, my temporary coworker, a portly white woman who looked like she'd reared five hearty boys, asked if I wanted to join her for a drink. Going drinking with colleagues after a long workday wasn't an experience I had often (unless my client wanted me to pretend to be a coworker), but it had been a stressful day, and I would likely never see this woman again, so I said sure, why not, and we rode the bus a short distance to a bar in Astoria where the dim, beer-fueled haze was a welcome reprieve from the sleet outside.

Over two rounds of stouts, the woman told me that she'd gotten into this kind of gig work as a way to escape from the mundanities of being a housewife (three boys, a dog, and a cat—I was close) and how fun it was for her to fill seats at award ceremonies and wait on lines for others. "It's as if I'm living another life," she said. "One where I get to attend these parties, even if I'm standing on the outside." She scratched her nose. "Not that I dislike my own life, of course. I love my kids, my pets, my husband. It's just nice to get out of the house every once in a while."

As we split the check, I asked her if she'd ever pretended to be someone else's mother for a gig.

"Like if they needed a mother-in-law or something?" she said.

"I was thinking more, like, for a child," I clarified, icing the crook of my elbow with my cool, empty mug.

"No way." She grimaced into the bottom of her glass. "I've read articles about other rentals who do stuff like that—they're the ones giving us a bad name! Call me old-fashioned, but pretending to care about an innocent child when you don't actually give a damn? Pardon my French, but that's just fucked-up. I could never pretend to be another child's mother. It'd feel like betraying my own kids."

I told her I agreed wholeheartedly, and we parted ways, her back to her full house, and me to mine. For the fifth day in a row, I began drafting an email to Lily, but caught myself nodding off at my desk, jaws tight from clenching. It seemed that the vortex energy of an airport during the holidays had drained even me—who had no plans to fly anywhere.

That night I dreamed of a conversation with Darlene that we'd had a few days ago about a short story she was writing, but this time we were in my Westlake apartment in LA and she looked different, eyes hooded with a drawn-on beauty mark high on her left cheek. The story too had changed. She said, Once upon a time in a poor village there was a little boy who had no friends except for his dog, who followed him everywhere. The dog knew when the boy was sad and when the boy was angry and when the boy said he wanted to be left alone but really wanted company. One day the boy's family had to go out of town and the boy left his dog with his relatives. It was a weekend trip and when the boy returned his relatives served him and his parents a meat dish. The boy hadn't eaten meat in months. He ate happily before realizing that he should save a bite for his dog. But of course, his dog was nowhere to be found. The end.

Do you get it? said dream Darlene. Do you get the point of the story?

No, I said, I don't get it.

Everyone betrays you in the end.

When I woke up I opened my phone to check when Darlene had scheduled our next meeting as we were seeing each other at least twice a week at this point. Mostly we chatted about life and art and literature, and I thought she might get a kick out of my dream. Maybe it would even inspire her writing, and I could feel as though I'd coauthored a story. But then I saw that she'd canceled our next two meetups, including one for tomorrow. The gaps in my schedule were disconcerting—had something happened? Should I reach out? The last message between us had been a *good night* from her the evening of the zoo meeting with Lily. I hadn't responded. I typed *Everything okay?* and then deleted it, replacing it with *Please cancel at least 24 hours in advance next time.* Hit send.

On Tuesday afternoon, before accompanying an older woman to the seven thirty showing of an opera, I finally sat down and wrote an email to Lily from her aunt starting with *I'm sorry it took me a while to write . . .* and ending with *Much love, your aunt, Darlene.* In the middle was an apology for not sending along a chapter of the memoir just yet; as the delay in email writing indicated, that was going to take me some time to draft. Darlene hadn't responded to my message, and in the worst moments I imagined her hooked up to several tubes, like a cephalopod in a hospital bed, but more likely, and hopefully, she was buckling down on her short story collection. In that case, I pictured her holed up in her apartment, sitting on a pillow on the floor, back against the wall, laptop balanced on her knees as she typed away, occasionally taking swigs from a liter bottle of chardonnay. Since she was well-off, the apartment would be large, but since she wasn't the type to know what to do with money anyway (a malady unique to those born rich), it would also be empty. Maybe a coffee table, a bed, a bookshelf. Maybe her being busy was a blessing in disguise. I was beginning to think too much about the fact she'd said we were friends, and truthfully, I missed her company.

I'd seen *The Magic Flute*, a holiday favorite among the sixty-and-up well-heeled female crowd, twenty-eight times, and so spent those two hours mentally working on a memoir by Darlene that would feature me in an innocuous way: the usual misgivings about the birth of a younger sibling, the visits from me at the hospital throughout her childhood, a jealousy of my freedom intermixed with sisterly care. And it had to be dark, since Darlene had said it would be, but what was appropriate for a ten-year-old? Unflinching descriptions of invasive tests and loose stools? Blood, bowels, and pain? Maybe I would send Lily what would be a later chapter in the book, full of hope for the future. A preachy, Chicken Soup for the Soul kind of writing to dull the pain of living and loss, flattening the future into one long road of "it gets better," as though life's only purpose was striving for more and better—forward and onward. Luckily the writing didn't actually need to be publishable; it didn't even have to be good. But I wanted it to shine. I wanted Lily to be proud of her aunt's writing, to believe that talent could run in the family and that the baton had already passed on to her.

After the show, I switched my phone back on and logged on to the fake email account for Darlene. Lily had responded to my earlier email, though it was not the answer I expected.

Hello, she wrote. *Is this your other email address?* And then, in a follow-up email as though this were a text message conversation: *I read the story you sent me and I think it's really sad that the little boy doesn't know that his family is tricking him . . .* And then, a third: *It was good though!! Your writing is compelling!!! I think I'm using that word right!* And finally, *Are you going back to LA? I thought we were hanging out this weekend?*

Someone had been contacting Lily as her aunt, and there was only one possibility.

I opened the Rental Stranger app and messaged Darlene. *Meet me, now.* The Darlene in my imagination, the one holed up in her room, morphed. She still sat in her bare apartment, back against a wall, laptop propped on her knees, but on her screen, instead of a short story, there was a draft of an email to Lily. This Darlene saw the message light up the phone by her side, read it, smiled that disconcerting smile of hers, and replied, *Well hello there, Stranger. Thought you'd never ask.*

CHAPTER 25

We met at a café on the Upper West Side. The nondescript doorway, squashed between a smoke shop and a falafel joint, led upstairs to a refined coffee shop where they served pour-overs and whisked matcha. That was the thing with New York—walking through these closet-sized doorways was always disorienting, like stumbling into Narnia time and time again. Though I'd lived my entire adult life in this city, I could never guess what was on the inside of buildings, and every time I was invited into a home I was baffled by what grand apartments hid behind unassuming facades and what hovels resided within ornate exteriors. In California, what you saw on the outside was what you got on the inside, every time.

When Darlene entered the café in her oversized brown jacket, curly hair tucked into an olive-green scarf, I felt tension's fist release me for a moment—an ungluing of the tongue, ungripping of teeth— before the shudder of rage overtook me. I was angry, yes, very angry that Darlene had reached out to Lily without my knowledge.

As she sat down and began unwrapping her scarf, I opened my mouth, but then realized that I had no idea how to advocate for myself—I was an expert in helping others achieve what they wanted, so much so that I never bothered to champion my own feelings. I was splitting again, seeing the situation from all sides. Was it so wrong that Darlene, a fake aunt, was communicating with Lily, my fake daughter? I was the one who'd conjured this relationship into being—I had no moral high ground and Darlene was even providing her services for free. So why the feeling of rage, then? It didn't seem like Darlene had said anything to hurt my relationship with Lily, at least not yet.

I swallowed. I'd been in such a rush to confront her that I hadn't thought through exactly what I'd say, or how. I didn't write anything out, nor did I practice in front of the mirror as I normally would have, so it was only hitting me now that this anger I felt might not have been wholly on Lily's behalf. Was I using Lily as an excuse?

Darlene wasn't harming Lily; she was hurting me. I was upset that Darlene would contact Lily without telling me, because, embarrassingly, somewhere along the way, I'd begun to believe that Darlene and I were on the same side, that she cared about me—not as a rental, but as a person. That we were friends. She had said so, and I believed her.

"Something to drink?" asked the server.

"No thanks," said Darlene.

"A matcha latte," I said.

After writing down my order, the server moved away with a slight bow toward me. I watched him take the order of the table adjacent to us. There was no bowing to the non-Asian couple.

Darlene fiddled with a strand of hair. "So?" she said with a smile. "You wanted to meet?"

"Why are you doing this to Lily?" I asked without preamble. Even though I could admit to myself this wasn't really about Lily,

I was still unable to say what I wanted to say: Why are you doing this to *me*?

"What do you mean?" said Darlene.

"Why are you emailing her? Arranging to meet with her?"

"Oh," said Darlene, "that's what this is about."

"Yes," I said, "what did you expect?"

"Nothing, nothing," she said, with a shrug, the self-sure smile still lingering.

I wanted to mirror her smile—I'd practiced plenty after watching her forfeit the chess match in Union Square Park. But I couldn't do it—I didn't have the confidence in knowing where this was going.

"I thought you might be happy," said Darlene. "With us playing family together. It was fun, wasn't it, that afternoon? I like the kid, you know?"

That afternoon at the zoo had been a surprisingly smooth few hours on the job, but it also radiated a warmth that I seldom felt in my life—the comfort of being in the company of two people who I'd known beyond a day, who were meeting for the first time and finding joy in each other. A whole afternoon spent with people who I believed cared about me, too. When had that ever happened before?

"It was a onetime thing," I said, taking back control of the encounter. "We agreed that I was going to email her afterward as you."

"Did we?" she said. "I don't remember agreeing to that."

Had I remembered wrong? I couldn't have left such a large variable up to Darlene.

"At the very least," I said, repositioning myself, "you were going to return to California within the week, not stick around to meet again."

"You got me there," said Darlene with a chuckle. She wasn't asking how I knew about her emails with Lily. Could it be that she wasn't trying to hide it? I could tell Darlene was thinking by the way she picked at her nails. She'd done that during the chess game too, picking at the grime beneath the crescent of her thumb before making the move that had led to her forfeiting. Was she feeling cornered, or amused? I couldn't tell. Of all the people I'd ever worked with, Darlene was the hardest to read. With her, even the most outlandish outcome was possible: like that she'd been excited I'd asked her to meet up because she was developing feelings for me. It wasn't so unlikely—this regularly happened with clients I met more than once. People often conflated kindness with love. In those instances, I gently reminded them that our relationship was an act. The man they envisioned, the man they named, was nothing more than a fiction of love.

"This might be out of left field," I said, "but you don't have feelings for me, do you? This whole Lily thing isn't just a way to get my attention, is it?"

Darlene's smile dissipated, and the somber affect made her face almost beautiful.

"Let's cut to the chase," she said. "You need to tell Lily that you're not her father."

I laughed. I couldn't help myself. It was such a ridiculous statement coming from Darlene, though she had never looked more serious.

"I'm not joking," she said. "It's not fair to her."

"And how would you know that, after meeting her once?"

"It's obvious!" said Darlene, loud enough that the couple next to us glared. She lowered her voice to a husky whisper. "You're the only one who doesn't see it."

"Doesn't see what?"

"That this whole thing is terrible for Lily. That she'll never know the love of a real father because you're there and yet not there."

"Oh? And what makes you an expert on child psychology?"

Darlene crossed her arms and leaned back, looking down at me through hooded eyes. "I know," she said, "that what hurts a child most is indifference."

I couldn't control my face anymore. I sneered. What did Darlene know of indifference? Maybe her parents had sent her away to boarding school, but then she must have had teachers and RAs and a whole host of other people looking after her, tending to her the way only money can provide. Had her birthdays been forgotten? Questions ignored and pains uncomforted? Besides, none of that had hurt me—I'd been fine, hadn't I? Fed? Housed? Loved?

"Fuck you," I said. "You and your cushy life. You don't know indifference. You don't know shit. You're a void of a human being who doesn't have real drama of her own so you want to ruin other people's lives for material. You think you know this family better than I do? I've known them for eight years! Lily is fine and her mother is fine and I am fine and we don't need you, you privileged hack."

Darlene laughed, though her eyes stayed narrowed, flashing at me as though her queen and rook had cornered my king at last. "I'm disappointed," she said. "I once thought you might have a real heart in there, but I had a feeling this might be the case after you said you didn't love Lily. I had to find out, and I'm glad to know that this is who you really are beneath the 'I just want to make everyone happy' bullshit." She raked her curls away from her face. "You're mean," she said. "Cruel and calculating. You think you're better than the rest of us sad, lonely people, but you're not. In fact, you're worse because you don't recognize how pathetic you really are. And the truth is, you aren't good enough for Lily. You don't deserve to keep a little girl from having a real, loving family. You're a fake, a fraud. And if you don't tell her the truth before this weekend, then I will."

"You'd ruin a little girl's life for your selfish ideals?" I said, gripping the table's edge.

"Oh please," said Darlene. "Look in a mirror."

I bolted up, surprising the server and causing him to spill the mug of matcha into his tray. I barely cut him a glance; my vision was crowded with Darlene—her hair static with anger, mouth twisted. Her eyes, though, looked strangely pained.

"You don't know me," I spit through clenched teeth. Unable to spend a single second longer with this woman who I'd foolishly believed to be my friend, I left the café: without apologizing, without paying, without a single thought in my head.

CHAPTER 26

On Thursday afternoon, while my arms automatically pulled on a flannel shirt, my mind snagged on Darlene's words. I had no doubt she would follow through with her threat and reveal the so-called truth to Lily just so she could shatter a little girl's world, gleefully sweeping up the broken shards and refashioning them into a story. "Look at this hurt," she would say to her readers, holding up the orb refracting the light with its jagged edges. "Doesn't it feel real?" The moment Darlene revealed herself to be a writer, I should have run the other way. It was unnatural to sit and invent on a page all day; when my mother shifted her time from acting to writing, I had been right to feel revolted. Seeing my mother write instead of act was like watching a bear walk on its hind feet and beg.

At the school gate, Piri and Lily walked out hand in hand, and this time, when I walked by Lily's side—reaching my hand out toward hers—she did not grab my fingers as usual. Instead, she looked straight ahead, her hand still squarely in Piri's as she swung her arm contentedly. She was quieter than usual, but Piri happily filled the space with his chatter.

I still had time before Darlene spoke to Lily, and that morning I had formulated a plan. I wasn't going to tell Lily about the rental agreement—there was no way—but I would come clean to Mari about Darlene's threats. Together, we could make sure that Darlene and Lily never met again, and that Lily blocked any incoming emails from Darlene. In order to make this worth Mari's while, I would finally propose what I'd decided: that there didn't need to be an off-boarding anytime soon and that I could become a permanent and more frequent fixture in their lives. Payment, if there needed to be payment, would be annual.

As the kids settled into their usual spots at the kitchen table, I poured two cups of guava juice and sat across from them. They both looked up at me at the same time, already in sync with their movements. When I didn't say anything, they lowered their heads back down and began their history homework—Piri was now able to sit still for long enough to fill out a questionnaire on ancient Egyptians. The second part of my plan involved speaking with Lily, but Piri wasn't going anywhere this afternoon, so anything I conveyed would have to be said in his presence. I scratched the crook of my elbow where my stress rash was now angrily spreading again.

"About your aunt," I said, testing the water.

"Yeah?" said Lily.

"The truth is, she's not well."

"I know," said Lily. "She said she had, um, some gastronomical disease."

"Wow," said Piri, "that's big."

"Gastrointestinal," I said, "but no, the thing is, she's actually not well in here." I pointed to my temple. "So it's better not to believe everything she says."

"She lies?" said Lily.

"She doesn't mean to, but she has delusions," I said. "As in, she can't always tell what's real from what's not real."

"Oh," said Lily, looking around at her objective reality—the kitchen where we sat and the living room with its taped couch, the carpet littered with library books, papers, socks, and takeout boxes. I hadn't yet had time to clean. "That's sad."

"Yes," I said, "it is."

"Your aunt's crazy?" said Piri. "I have a crazy uncle—I heard he would eat dirt and stuff and, like, one time he had to have surgery cuz he swallowed a razor and it cut his throat from the inside."

Lily winced.

"She's not that bad," I said. "But maybe for now, just, uh, keep your distance."

Lily nodded thoughtfully and I waited for her to tell me that she had originally made plans with her aunt this weekend, but would cancel now that she knew her aunt wasn't to be trusted. But Lily said nothing.

"You don't have plans to meet with her, do you?" I asked.

"Nope," said Lily, looking down at a diagram of Egyptian laborers rolling bricks up a ramp to construct the pyramids. I knew she was lying but what could I say? That I'd pretended to be her aunt and knew what they were emailing about? I was the one who taught her that lying was okay. It was time for plan B. I would have to ask Mari to stop Lily from going out to meet her aunt this weekend.

When Mari returned home, she said nothing about how I hadn't yet finished making dinner, or how the dining table was still sticky where Piri had spilled some juice. Instead, she cracked open a can of beer, asking Lily how her day was. She was more alive and attentive than I'd seen in weeks.

"Good day at work?" I asked, ladling chicken soup over rice and bringing it to the dinner table.

Mari looked away, but couldn't hide a smile. "I guess," she said. And then, "Well, I got a new job."

"That's great news!" I said. But based on the way she sucked in her lips I could tell there was more to it. "And?"

"That's it," she said. "It's thanks to my new boss. A good guy."

"Michael," said Lily, looking at me meaningfully.

"You know him?" I asked.

"No," said Lily, "but Mom's been talking about him a lot. They've been, like, meeting up."

"Ah," I said, feeling Lily's eyes trained on me. I remembered then that she'd been trying to tell me something along these lines at Fort Washington Park before we'd had the run-in with the nosy blonde. Was this it? That there was a rift in her family, another man in the picture, and she wasn't sure what her dad was going to do about it? Was she worried that he would be hurt or was she worried that he wouldn't seem to care at all? Perceptive as she was, history informed her it was probably the latter. Indifference: Darlene's accusation pointed its finger at me. I hadn't anticipated another man when formulating my plans this morning—I'd been off my game lately. I should have noticed the signs of an interloper far earlier. I thought Mari had been distracted by work stress, but instead she had been shifting allegiances—falling in love. Had she been testing me when she asked if I wanted to know why she wasn't picking Lily up from school lately? If I'd said yes, if I'd shown hurt or jealousy, would she have stopped seeing him? I shoveled a big spoonful of soup and rice into my mouth. Chewed. Swallowed. "He must be good at his job," I said.

"Yup," said Mari, shooting a look at Lily that clearly translated to: stop talking. "He sure is."

"I'm full," said Lily, pushing her chair away from the table.

"You should eat more," I said. She'd had all of two bites.

"I ate a lot for lunch," she said.

Usually, after each meal, Lily would help me wash the dishes, but tonight she beelined straight into the bedroom and closed the door. I knew that Lily was likely giving me the opportunity to speak with Mari "alone" as she pressed her ear against the door (did she want to hear a fight? Was silence the void of love?), but I felt paralyzed. I'd failed to consider this angle in my plans and now what would I say to Mari? Forget this guy? Choose me? Pathetic. I pushed out my chair to get up and wash the dishes alone.

"Wait," said Mari. "I was thinking . . ."

And I knew what she'd been thinking before she said it. Mari, unlike Darlene, was fully scrutable, and had my mind not been occupied by the Darlene-Lily debacle, I would have noticed the signs earlier. In all the years I'd known her, I'd never seen Mari wear eyeliner, never heard her call any man "a good guy." In Mari's life, men were either assholes or doormats, and she had no use for either. She was too focused on providing for Lily to have time for something as frivolous as love; in that way, I'd thought we were similar. Dedicated workers. But now it seemed that Mari was leaving me behind. What was so great about this Michael guy that he could wedge his way into Mari's heart?

"Is this about your new boss?" I said.

"Yes," she said, a slight flush to her cheeks that I hadn't seen since the first few Christmases we'd spent together as a family. Mari wasn't mine, but I didn't realize how much I'd hate to see her pining after someone else.

"He might just be acting nice, you know, to a new hire." I was oddly vulnerable sitting in my pushed-out chair, too far from the table to hide my fidgeting hands.

"Actually," Mari said, "I've known him for almost a year now. We were coworkers at my old job. He was always cheering me up until he left for his new workplace six months ago. I ran into him again recently and told him about the terrible new boss and he, well, he helped me get hired, so I really owe him. Like I said, he's a good guy."

"You know," I said, "it's not a great idea to get too friendly with your boss." My head felt fizzy, and like a shaken-up soda the pressure was building inside me. I gripped the edge of my seat to stop from swaying.

Mari's face shifted from a rosy flush to fully red. "I didn't say that I was—" she said. "Only that he's—oh, I don't know!"

I saw an opening and dropped my voice so that Lily couldn't hear. "It's dangerous to mix pleasure and business—think about it. What if you date and you begin to dislike the way he leaves dirty socks all over the apartment for you to step on like crumpled cow pies? Then what can you say to him? He's your boss. If you make him mad, he might make your working life miserable. And if you break up, you'll lose your job. It's too dangerous."

"He's not like that," said Mari, but I could see the doubt in her eyes.

"That's why we should stick together," I said, still feeling like I could float away with the slightest word. "You know I won't leave. In fact . . ." I tried to stand, but decided it was safer to stay seated. I scooted my chair back to the table. "I was thinking of staying on long term," I said, leaning forward, "if that's okay with you."

"Long term . . ." said Mari, fingers tracing the condensation ringing the beer can, circle after circle. This was the first time that I'd ever stated what I wanted out of our relationship, and I could see she was considering what I'd proposed, so I pressed forward.

"If we change to a long-term model, I'm thinking that the payments could be annually instead of hourly and we could even draw up our own contract—it doesn't have to be on the app. That way I could spend more time with Lily and with you, of course, if you don't mind. I'll tell Lily that my job now has me on shorter drives so I can be home more often. Maybe three times a week, even! That way we could be more of a family, you know? Of course, we can discuss what kind of annual fee makes sense, but I'll make sure it's fair and affordable."

"Wow," said Mari, pinching her bottom lip with her fingers. "That's . . ."

I could see that she was weighing options in her mind: me vs. Michael. I needed, due to time constraints, to tell Mari about Darlene, but I was afraid that it would tip the scales in Michael's favor.

"That's great," she said. "Or, I guess that would have been great. Oh God, this is hard."

I got up and put a hand on her shoulder, hoping that she wouldn't feel that I was shaking. "Let's go talk about it outside."

Out on the stoop, in the solid dark, both of us bundled in our jackets. Mari lit her cigarette. The darkness shifted. I took a deep breath, letting the cool night air settle me down.

"There is one thing," I said, "that you need to know."

"Mhmm," said Mari, looking down the street toward the fruit cart vendor beneath the flickering streetlamp, packing away his wares for the evening, the same guy who was always there, always packing up when I left, every Thursday, without fail.

"The aunt that I introduced Lily to, well, she's contacting Lily via email and they have plans to meet this weekend. I think it's best if you cut off their communication. Block her email address and don't let Lily see her."

Mari's head snapped back toward me. "What?"

"I said—"

"No, no," said Mari. "I heard what you said. Lily's been talking to some stranger?"

"She's not a stranger," I said. "She's an . . . acquaintance of mine, but it's best if Lily doesn't meet her again."

"And why's that?" said Mari.

"She's . . ." A hundred different excuses and lies passed through my mind, but this was Lily's life, and Mari deserved to know the truth. I hoped that Mari would recognize this as a sign of my trustworthiness. "She's threatening to reveal that I'm a rental."

Mari's eyes widened, reminding me of the mouse in the freezer, trapped in a cup of ice—bewildered and unbelieving that everything it had ever known could simply one day cease.

"You let my little girl meet someone who could undo everything?"

"Truthfully," I said, "I didn't know she was like that, until recently."

"That's even worse!" said Mari.

"It was a mistake," I said.

"I don't pay you to make mistakes," said Mari.

"I know," I said. "I apologize. It won't happen again."

"You apologize? You promised me everything would be okay! How is this okay?"

"It's not," I said.

"So then what?"

The look in her eyes was earnest in its pleading, as though I, who'd trapped her, could also set her free. Yes, if Mari was the mouse, then I was my mother finding the poor creature in the snow—I understood, in that moment, why she'd scooped that animal into a cup and kept it nearby, forever frozen.

"Well," I said, scratching at the crook of my elbow. I noticed Mari's eyes narrow in on this motion, her mind now susceptible to fabricating other horrible secrets I'd been hiding, wondering what kind of man she'd allowed into her home all these years, let near her child—just him and her, alone. "It's just a rash," I said.

Mari ground out her half-smoked cigarette beneath her feet, her face shrouded without its glow. "No more," she said.

I choked on my inhale; the breath lodged somewhere behind my Adam's apple, refusing to enter my lungs. Neither of us looked at the other. We didn't have to. I knew what expression her face would hold. After all these years together, I sensed the parentheticals around her mouth deepening, eyes blinking slowly: the face she made every time she arrived at an irrefutable decision.

"Hold on," I said.

"Please," she said, "just leave."

"It's a solvable problem," I said. "A small hiccup—not a big deal."

"Not a big deal?" said Mari. "You think fucking up my daughter's life isn't a big deal?"

"That's not what I meant!" I said. "It's just that—this aunt issue is something we can contain, and then it'll be as though it never happened. If I leave now, our little girl will—"

"Stop it," she said. "Don't call her *our little girl* when it's convenient for you."

"Please," I said, "she needs me."

"No," said Mari. "She doesn't need you. We don't need you. I should've done this a long time ago, but I was too insecure, and you—" She ran her hand through her graying hair. "You prey off people's insecurities. You don't let them change or grow. You want them to be weak, to depend on people like you—making us think you're the answer, when in reality, you're a damn parasite, and I was too stupid to see it."

"That's not true," I said. "All I want is for you to be happy."

"Okay then," she said. "If that's all you want, leave."

I took a step back to hold on to the brick wall that I was so familiar with. Eight years of entering and exiting this building. There was no way this was the end. Right now, Lily was upstairs, wondering

KAT TANG

when I would come back in with her mother. Yes, it was a fight—
but didn't fighting mean that there was a connection worth fighting
over? At worst I wouldn't return tonight, but I would return in a
week—because that was what I did. I was here: week after week
after week. So what would happen when I didn't show? Would she
blame herself? Would she think that maybe—if she hadn't been sullen over dinner, if she'd washed the dishes with me, hadn't made a
scene—then I would have stayed?

"Let me at least say something to Lily," I said. And then, reframing:
"Closure is important for cognitive development. Otherwise Lily might
learn unhealthy attachment styles due to abandonment trauma."

For a moment Mari uncrossed her arms, trying to parse if what
I'd said made sense, but then she closed her eyes. Let out a long-held
breath. Shook her head.

"No more of your bullshit," she said as she turned and let herself
into the building, shutting the door behind her.

I punched the wall. My knuckles throbbed but the wall remained
unchanged. This couldn't be it. This couldn't be over. I should run
back in there and try to convince Mari to let me stay. Please. Because it was so clear to me now that my happiest moments were the
handful of hours on Thursdays I spent with Lily, watching her grow
up, basking in the enjoyment she felt in my presence. But if I finally
acknowledged how much I liked the feeling of being needed—not
just for a few hours, or a few days, but for a lifetime; and that without her, no one would notice or care if I was gone—now that I could
finally admit this to myself, didn't that mean I'd broken my biggest
rule of no emotional attachment?

What was the penalty for defying a self-imposed rule? What
were the consequences?

CHAPTER 27

The next morning, I attended a wake in Greenwich Village. I was still reeling from the events of the previous night, and the overly perfumed room threatened to strangle what little air I had left in my lungs, when I recognized a black-clad figure. The old man, who'd been my father at the wedding in Connecticut, was loitering around the edges of the room. When he left the funeral home—for a smoke, I figured, by the way he kept licking his lips and patting his leather jacket pocket—I followed. Out on the street, shop windows were strung with lights and decorated with tinseled mini-trees and animatronic penguins singing carols. Steam billowed from a manhole.

"Bum a smoke?" I said, standing by the old man's side.

He glanced at me and passed over the pack.

"I'll take you up on your offer now," I said, both jittery and tense, like I could shake myself apart.

"Dunno what you're talking about," said the old man. He'd modulated his voice for this role, sounding like he smoked four packs a day and ashed his cigarettes in Johnnie Walker.

"Can I get a light?"

I wasn't much of a smoker, but for the moment, the taste of to-
bacco on my tongue and the hit of nicotine to my brain helped me
ignore the dread weighing me down.

"What do you do when you get attached to someone?" I asked.

The old man frowned as he removed the cigarette from his
mouth, inspecting it as though it had turned rancid. "You don't,"
he said.

"And if it's already happened?"

"Then you leave."

A crowd of twenty-somethings dressed in Santa outfits swung
plastic bottles of alcohol above their heads like bells as they crashed
into one another. They smelled, collectively, of Baileys.

"But what if they miss me when I leave?"

"Miss you?" the old man said, jamming the cigarette back into
the corner of his mouth. "Who," he said, taking a long pull, "are you?"

I couldn't answer.

"Let me tell you a tale," said the old man. "Once upon a time, I
was married. I was in my forties, but nothing in my wild youth had
given me lasting happiness, so I thought, yeah, why not, give domes-
tic bliss a shot. So we got married, and we had a daughter, and I was
happy. But I found out after a couple o' years that happiness grated
on me. It was work, and it was exhausting. I was exhausted. And
that's when I realized the truth: happiness doesn't exist. It's that
simple! So rather than pursuing some bullshit idea, I decided to give
up pretending for free. You want my help in pretending happiness
exists? You pay for it. Easy as that."

"But what if I were to stay?" I said, unable to swallow the acrid
spit pooling in my mouth. "What if I told her the truth, you know,
that I do care about her—as more than just a client?"

He rolled up his jacket sleeves, crossed his arms. "Do whatever you want—but remember, people like us aren't capable of love. You might think you care now, but just wait a few years. You'll only hurt 'em worse. We. Don't. Know. How. To. Stay. That's what makes us so good at what we do. So keep doing what you're good at, and leave the happy pretenders to their own game." With that, he walked back inside to do what he'd been doing for decades—act like he cared for people he didn't give two shits about.

The app on my phone buzzed, letting me know my time as a mourner was over.

I crushed my burnt-out cigarette beneath my heel. The nicotine high had already dissipated.

I wouldn't be like him.

CHAPTER 28

I checked the time: Lily would be getting out of school in about two hours, and I could get changed and head uptown in far less time than that. I didn't have a plan—at least, not the usual kind. Rather than relying on words or actions, today, I was betting on emotion. I had to believe that the love I held for Lily, and she for me, would somehow win over Mari. That was how it worked in the movies, wasn't it? If my dedication were strong enough, then the happy outcome would be inevitable. And we could all continue on as we had before.

As I rushed down Canal Street, however, I was shocked to see a man I recognized through a dim sum shop window. I stopped in my tracks. Here before me was the very first person I'd ever worked for as a rental. Was this a sign? I needed to ask him: was he still happy? I stared and he stared back. We stood, unblinking, peering at one another, until I realized that I was looking at myself—only washed out like the faded images of har gow and egg tarts, my features slightly warped by the reflective restaurant window. I was amazed by how much I looked like him now. Ten years later, I'd grown to possess the same furrowed brows and harried features of the man who'd unwittingly started me on the Rental Stranger path: Curtis Kawamoto, MD.

On one of the many hazy days after my mother's suicide—when I had no guidance for my own future, and the long, unwavering New York City streets taunted me with their steadfastness—Curtis had caught sight of me in a midtown café. We stared at our own dopple-ganger: me, in my white T-shirt, with a turkey sub raised halfway to my mouth; and him, in his scrubs, and five o'clock shadow at two in the afternoon. His first words to me were as efficient as those of a man who knew his time was worth people's lives.

"How would you like to make some money?"

"Do I know you?" I'd asked, disturbed by how similar we looked—like staring into a crystal ball and seeing your future.

"No," he'd said.

"But we look—"

"We both just have one of those faces," he said. "Only so many ways for Asian and white to mix."

I glanced down at his clogs, spotting a dark stain on the left one. "I'm not selling my organs," I said.

He laughed, a sharp sound that conveyed amusement but not joy. "It's an easy job. The person who did it before bailed, but I'll pay you a hundred and fifty per hour."

"What is it?" I asked.

"It's simple," he said. "All you have to do is be me."

It was my first assignment, and I remembered the walk to the West Village, avoiding the poops of small dogs (it was always the small poops, as though dog owners thought that below a certain size the turd would simply melt away), and finding a brownstone where I took the stoop steps two at a time, squishing browned magnolia petals beneath my feet. I double-checked the building number and rang the bell.

An old woman in a floral-print muumuu answered the door after a long pause. She was hunched over and peeked her head up like a turtle, squinting against the sunlight.

"Hello?" she said, her English heavily accented, adding vowels to the ends of words. "Can I help you?"

"It's me, Curtis," I said, suddenly feeling foolish and hot in the face.

"Ka-ti-su," said the old woman, taking such care with her grandson's name that it came out in three syllables. "お久しぶりです."

Curtis had explained that his grandmother suffered from dementia, so there was no way she could tell me from the last guy pretending to be him—as though my goal were not to be Curtis himself but to impersonate an impersonator. "And if she says she doesn't know who you are, just remind her that she's not all the way there," he'd said, pointing to his head. Despite being a doctor, Curtis seemed to have no qualms gaslighting the elderly. Or perhaps this was what happened when you treated patients day after day after day—you triaged, even when they were family.

Walking down the long, dark hallway of the grandmother's apartment was like traversing the pages of an *I Spy* book: wallpaper with flowers the color of coffee stains, covered at random by dusty framed photographs, while tchotchkes smothered every horizontal surface. I pretended to be interested in the array of porcelain animals to avoid the woman's gaze.

"Coffee?"

"Sure," I said, taking advantage of any opportunity for her to not look me in the face. When she returned, balancing two cups of steaming coffee on a tray, I jumped up to help.

"お座り," she said.

I stood awkwardly, unsure of what to do.

"Sit," she said, motioning to a well-worn green loveseat.

I sat. Curtis hadn't mentioned foreign language skills in the job description. But certainly now, this woman would know that I wasn't her grandson if I couldn't even speak the language she'd probably spoken to him since birth. But the way she looked at me—kind, gentle, without reproach—made me realize that she was not as far gone as Curtis thought she was.

"So, Curtis," she said, "tell me about you."

It hit me that Curtis, who likely hadn't seen his grandmother in a long time, did not know that this woman was well aware that his stand-ins were not her actual grandson. And yet she didn't seem to care. She was grateful for the company and kept up the charade because she was lonely. I wondered if the previous Curtis had realized this—and quit once he began feeling bad for this lonely woman. Maybe he thought that by quitting, the real Curtis would come and pay his grandmother a visit. But even after a short interaction, I knew Curtis would never visit. And for a hundred and fifty dollars an hour, I wouldn't make the same mistake as my predecessor.

After three hours—during which her eyes did sometimes glaze over, and she would speak for long stretches of time in a language I could not understand—the woman's voice began to give out.

"Come tomorrow?" she said. I glanced around the dark interior of this home—ebony wood furnishings gave it a feeling of antiquated luxury, but dust had settled everywhere, including on the crowns of hundreds of porcelain elephants painted in fading blues and pinks and grays. The shag carpet smelled musky, as if it had been there since Curtis's grandmother was a young woman—perhaps newly in love, or pregnant with the child who would become the father to a boy who'd grow up to hire strangers to pretend to be him.

"Of course," I said.

Was it so burdensome to have a grandmother? I had no idea. I liked listening to her—though I hoped all the stories she told in a language I couldn't understand weren't any good, so that they weren't wasted on me.

When I stepped out of her brownstone and onto the streets, New York City seemed a little brighter. A frizzy-haired woman laden with shopping bags passed by, swearing as the handles dug into her palms. I wondered if she would hire someone to be her friend, to carry her bags when she went shopping in the morning, then comb out the knots in her hair in the afternoon while gossiping about lost love. And the elderly man across the street coming out of his brownstone, with bowed shoulders and his head down—perhaps he might want a son to come and check up on him every so often, so that he could tell the neighbors how loved he was, until he believed it himself. There were so many people who lived in this city with sickened hearts and diseased relationships. I could be a balm. I could become a brother, a lover, a son, a friend; I could make them happy. Luckily for me (as Curtis informed me, once we met up after the assignment) like everything else in this intensely connected yet deeply lonely life, there was an app for that.

All these years later, had I accomplished what I'd set out to do? Make people happy? I liked to think so. I liked to imagine that everyone I'd worked for was better off with my assistance than without. That was why I couldn't give up on Lily and Mari—not yet, not while Lily still needed me. If I could just speak with Lily, maybe I could convince her to convince her mother that I was the only father figure she needed—that gambling on this Michael guy was going to end in disaster.

*

Back in my apartment, I threw a sewing kit into my backpack, pulled on my father outfit, and then headed back out to Canal Street, where the oppressive cheeriness of the holidays attacked me from all sides. Luckily, a few steps into the subway station and all season's greetings were erased, as no one in the MTA was decorating the tiled walls. Down here, holidays manifested only in the form of a scantily dressed elf puking into a bag in the corner of a subway car. I claimed a seat by the door and then closed my eyes, willing the screeching of the rails to drown out my jumbled thoughts. Nevertheless, my mind assaulted me from all sides—playing out every possible outcome, even though I wanted to see only one: the one where I stayed. But what if everyone else was right? What if the best thing to do was to leave, and let Lily—and by extension, Mari—move on without me? What if any meaning that I'd given to their lives so far would be stifled by my continued presence?

Selfishly, no matter what happened, I wanted above all else to remain in Lily's memories as a good father, a trustworthy man. I'd finally practiced enough to competently fix a fraying hem but hadn't had the chance to do so yet. Even though she was already outgrowing her skirts, if she wore them one last time when the weather turned warm again in the spring, she might remember me fondly. Or she might curse me. Either way, she would think of me.

At the school gates, I shifted my weight, feeling an unfamiliar tightening of my gut at the realization that I was here on my own and not by a client's request. I felt as though I were breaking the law—but when the bell rang, I pushed these worries aside. I couldn't imagine a life without Lily. I needed her; I hoped she felt the same way. As the kids streamed past me, I saw the top of Lily's head in the crowd. Piri was next to her, as always, and he whispered something into her ear, making her giggle. She was wearing the mustard-yellow coat again, which was now missing its top button.

She looked happy.

I realized at that moment that I'd often imagined Lily's face when she left school on the days when I wasn't there to pick her up. In my visions, she would search for me in the crowd, the way she did every Thursday. That even on a Wednesday or a Friday, when she knew I wouldn't be there, her disappointment would slink through despite her best efforts to hide it. But now I could see that she wasn't looking for me at all. She and Piri formed their own little world, and the possibility that I would be there by the school gates that day wasn't even on her radar. It was as though outside of Thursday afternoons I simply ceased to exist. Maybe I couldn't imagine a life without Lily, but she lived a whole life without me—she did it almost every day of the week. And it hit me then, the truth: no one needed me—not Darlene, not Mari, not even Lily. Had anyone needed me at all? Ever?

Piri, holding Lily's hand, walked right past me and I could see in his small frame how straight his back was, how squared his shoulders. Perhaps he could carry her burdens, and Lily would find herself attracted to this quality for the rest of her life: the dependability of those who stayed.

I watched as they walked away. I couldn't bring myself to follow. I could see myself now as though hovering above my own body: a strange man following two children back home, feeding them juice, cleaning their floors, mending their clothes. All I was doing was making myself useful so that I might be loved, but I was nothing but a leech simpering for a taste of adjacent happiness. I turned to face the school building, touching my forehead to its cool, rough surface. I laughed, or I cried. Maybe it was both. The tears were a release sweeter than any orgasm. And I knew, in that moment, what I had to do.

I opened the app to message a client off the clock—something that I never would've done a few months ago. But then again, I'd been breaking my own rules left and right—what did it matter to do so one last time?

You win, I wrote to Darlene.

I'm leaving. But if you ever see Lily again, please, don't tell her it was a lie.

It wasn't.

I do love her.

And then I went into my profile and pressed DELETE. Was I sure? YES. But what about my pre-existing client bookings—was I okay with canceling all future appointments? YES. But I wouldn't be able to retain my profile data, so was I really sure? YES. Really? YES.

With a final tap, nearly a decade of work—thousands of clients, all my five-star reviews, my entire life—dissipated.

Perhaps it was in my blood, passed down from father and mother, to leave those we were supposed to love.

I walked down the street and hailed a cab to take me home.

CHAPTER 29

Growing up in LA, I often had the impression that I was living in a simulation. On a perfect seventy-five-degree day in the dead of winter, when it was so temperate that my insides felt at equilibrium with the outside world, I would have the odd sensation that I was walking through nothing—or, worse, that I was nothing. The smog and sun buffed away the edges of reality. I would glance around at the other people on the street and wonder if they felt it too: that we were all playing programmed parts.

Now, from the balcony of the apartment I was renting, I watched the sun glitter along the edge of palm fronds and marveled at what a high-resolution simulation this was. Barely any pixelation at all.

For my first few days back in LA, I'd stayed inside the apartment I'd found on Craigslist—a sparsely furnished one bedroom on a quiet street near Venice Beach. There—bloated with self-loathing, but unable to do anything besides roll around on the collapsing twin bed—my finger hovered over the download button of the app ten times a day, but I couldn't go through with it. My profile was gone, erased. Anyone who tried to reach me would see an error message and a suggested list of other recommended rentals. Mostly I agonized about whether Mari would have tried to message me after realizing the mistake she'd made by telling me to go; but I knew, as well as I knew the contours of my own face, that her pride would never allow her to reach out to me again.

The nights were worse than the days. On my sixth night, I dreamt that Lily and I were sitting in Central Park, braiding white clovers into wreaths with needle and thread, though my thread kept snapping, its dangling ends threatening to unravel my creation. After a parade of dachshunds passed by, Lily tilted her head in my direction and informed me that she was angry, very angry with my falsehoods, but that after eating two slices of American Cheddar, she had decided that she could forgive me. When I held her in my arms, I knew, with certainty, that this was happiness. I woke with a start at five in the morning, still unadjusted to California time, and though my head felt waterlogged, I couldn't cry—the contrast between my dream and reality had scooped my heart clean out. It was after that dream that I decided to finally leave the apartment.

My first stop was the ocean, which was nearly at my doorstep. Then, I meandered through old neighborhoods I'd lived in as a child. LA was not a walking city, but I rather enjoyed the foot bridges perilously close to oncoming traffic and the sidewalks swallowed up by tent cities. A bit of danger during my waking hours meant that I needed to focus on the immediate present or else get run over by a Bentley driven by a fifteen-year-old.

Some moments I even felt a twisted pleasure at my aimlessness, marveling at how easy it was to leave everything behind. Even my apartment on Canal Street—which I'd been paying for month to month in cash, and where I'd accrued my whole life's work—could simply be abandoned for the landlord to clean out (and turn a profit by selling my goods secondhand). My only regret was that somewhere, amid the clutter, I'd left my mother's last note: the only piece of her I had left.

After a few days of walking, I developed a blister at the base of my big toe, but I didn't mind the way it chafed. I was grateful, also, for the exhaustion that took me each night. The dreamless sleep.

But all too soon, my body became accustomed to the walks, and my mind revved back up. When I was in a really punishing mood, I let myself envision what Lily must be thinking. What excuse could Mari possibly have made? That I was called away to a foreign land? Kidnapped, killed, enlisted, drowned, buried alive, lost in the woods, flown into the Bermuda Triangle? Or, that I was simply a no-good second-rate scoundrel who ran away? There was no doubt that Lily was devastated, that she missed me. But was there also a small part of her that felt relieved? A part of her that no longer had to question what her role was in her mother's and my "arrangement," or play the perfect daughter just so that I might stay? With her mother, she could bicker and express disappointment, but with me she was always so careful, and calm, and good. Now she didn't have to pretend anymore.

Every so often on my walks, I would catch someone staring at me; and though I'd been avoiding mirrors, I knew myself well enough to see what they saw: my hair unkempt and my stubble overgrown, stretched-out shirt and dusted jeans. Not a product I would buy, not anymore. I'd read that the creators of Rental Stranger were originally from LA, and when they'd first test piloted the program in New York City they'd brought over some thirty aspiring actors and actresses to play the parts. I wondered how those people had felt: transformed into human goods, as easily bought as rolls of toilet paper or Indian food. But it's not like that was anything new for society; being bought by the hour was, after all, the oldest profession.

Still, a hooker was a hooker and a mover a mover—but what were we? I'd once read an article online calling us "Scammers of the Coastal Elite," and maybe that was what some Rental Strangers did, but that wasn't what I'd wanted. I'd wanted my customers to be happy, and I'd wanted my mother to be happy. But I'd failed them just as I'd failed her.

On Sunset Boulevard I stumbled upon an antiques shop that had, in the display case beneath the register, a set of tools resembling an oxidized version of a middle schooler's geometry set. The woman behind the counter—the picture of a high school gym teacher, with her cropped alarm-red hair and full jogger suit—sensed my interest and informed me these were old cartography tools. She then proceeded to wax poetic about the era of imaginative mapmaking: European explorers filling the blanks in Africa and Asia with chimeric animals—pigs with fins, lions with human faces, a king riding a whale with horse legs! What an era it was! Mapmaking now had no imagination: a camera strapped to a car rendering life as it was, not as it could be.

When I handed her two hundred dollars in cash she said, "Xie xie."

I replied, "不客气" and she looked taken aback, as though I'd cursed at her.

On the bus ride home, I realized that I could no longer see Lily's face with absolute clarity in my mind's eye—was her hair the same shade as her pupils or her irises? Did she have a freckle above her left or right eyebrow? I pulled out my phone with its empty photo roll and opened the trash, determined to recover the photo taken at Grand Central of the two of us when we'd seemed invincible, but it had been more than thirty days, and the photos were gone, permanently erased. I looked up to see that I had missed my transfer stop and the bus was ambling north.

Clutching the metallic case with cartography tools inside, I exited and made my way west. West toward the ocean and west toward the country my mother had left when she was a young woman with a dream. There was no clear path for me now—no way to repent or atone. I felt as lost and afraid as I did the day my mother died: as though the years in between had melted and turned to slush, untenable as California snow.

CHAPTER 30

Late one afternoon, the week before Christmas, I found myself near the community center where my mother had taken acting classes. The benches of splintered green wood were the same ones I'd sat on while waiting for her to finish class—where I'd turned the cracked terrain into a jungle for my finger soldiers to traverse in order to save the princess trapped at the enemy base. My childhood was where war, Super Mario, and public benches intersected.

Had I ever been so satisfied as on those long afternoon days, lost in my own heroics, knowing that my mother was only a door's width away?

The entrance to the old acting classroom (still the same faded blue) was slightly ajar. I hadn't seen the place since I became a teenager and stopped accompanying my mother to her classes, but I could still picture the worn carpet, walls of bulletin boards tacked with competing class materials, chairs stacked in the corner. I had to know if things had changed. Poking my head in, even the smell of the place was familiar: nervous sweat, stale sunscreen, and chemical cleaner. It seemed that a class had ended recently, as the chairs were not stacked but arranged in a haphazard semicircle, and illegible notes remained scrawled on the blackboard.

"Hey!" came a woman's voice from behind me. "You're not supposed to be in there!"

I whipped around to see a middle-aged Asian woman with long, black hair and bangs cut just above the brows. For a moment, I thought *Mother*, and my legs nearly buckled. But as the woman walked closer, I saw that she was not nearly as beautiful as my mother had been—more of a droop to the edges of her eyes and the corners of her mouth, though the lips had clearly been injected with filler. Her top lip barely moved when she spoke.

"Wait a minute," she said. "Don't I know you?"

She didn't resemble any previous client of mine, but there wasn't anything that time and plastic surgery couldn't change. She wore a red tank top with a loose white blouse over it, tied above the waist so her belly button peeked out above denim cutoffs. It was an outfit that someone twenty years younger might wear, but she still had the figure for it.

"I have one of those faces," I said.

"No, no," she said, and then, snapping her fingers until her eyes lit up and she speared her finger at me. "I know! You're Anna's kid! Wow, you look just like her."

Anna. I hadn't heard that in years. My mother's English name. A perfect name, she'd said. The same backward and forward. Nothing to do with Anna May Wong. Mother would succeed where Anna May Wong had stumbled.

The woman whistled, low and slow as in a movie. "What's it been, like, ten years?"

"Closer to fifteen," I said with a tight-lipped smile. I hadn't expected to run into anyone familiar with my past or with my

214

mother—but why, then, was I walking around our old neighbor-hoods? Maybe it wasn't a haunting but a sleuthing. Maybe this was what I'd wanted but hadn't dared hope for.

"Fifteen years! Damn, that's a long time. Look, I forgot to lock up, so why don't I do that and then you and I can grab a drink and catch up."

I wasn't sure what we'd have to catch up on, considering I'd stopped waiting around on those green benches by the time I'd hit middle school. Maybe I'd seen her once or twice after that when I drove over to pick up my mother, but that had been so many years and faces ago. For some reason, I felt annoyed by this woman who was in front of me, breathing, talking, gesticulating. I didn't want to see her face so clearly when I couldn't even remember my own mother's. And what could she possibly want from me? Was she memorizing my every shuffle and grimace to report back to her friends about how far Anna's son had fallen? Would she secretly feel satisfied that my mother (whose talent and looks they were surely jealous of) had a son who wandered the streets of LA on a workday afternoon wearing a sweat-stained T-shirt and a pair of flip-flops he'd picked up from Walgreens?

But even now, as she chattered on about The Good Old Days while scrounging in her oversized purse for a set of keys (as though I cared about how cheap gas was back then), I didn't detect any mal-ice, and so I eased back into myself. This was a good opportunity to learn about my mother from someone who remembered her. Un-fortunately, the woman wasn't giving me any chance to ask a single question. She finally interrupted her own monologue with an "aha!" as she pulled out the keys to lock the door, but then, within the same breath, launched into the roster of who'd made it and who'd failed coming out of their community acting classes. She artfully did not mention my mother in her list of those who hadn't reached renown. I'd seen clients ramble like this before. She was nervous. But why?

"There's a bar around the corner," she said. "Dive, so, no dress code," she added with a glance at my disheveled clothes.

"Sounds good," I said.

At the bar (which looked like it had taken one glance at a Dive Bar template and said "That'll do") we slid into a corner booth. I paid for my beer in cash and offered to pay for her double G&T, which she happily accepted. My forearms stuck to the table as I twisted the plastic cup around and around.

"I'm sorry," I said, "but I forgot your name."

"Theresa," she said. "It was Theresa Walcott for a while but now it's back to Theresa Lang. Isn't that funny? As a kid, you dream about changing your name to Mrs. Redford, but you never think about how you'll want to change it back after the divorce. And the paperwork! So many things and places that have your name attached to them, you know?" I did know. I tried to avoid all of them. "Banks, the IRS, licenses, bills, alumni registries, voter registries, insurance, doctors, the post office, mailing lists, credit cards, food delivery apps . . ."

Theresa wasn't my client, and it wasn't my job to make her feel more at ease, but years of habit didn't just end in a few weeks. To help her relax, I told her, "Theresa Lang has a nice ring to it."

"Tell that to the casting directors," she said, pushing her straw away from her face with the back of her index finger as she drank from the side of her cup. "Definitely got more gigs as a Walcott. Though, obviously, nothing really panned out. God, it's great to see you and all, but what a reminder that after so many years, what have I managed to do? Move from acting student to acting teacher. And get a divorce. Sheesh. How's your mother doing?"

"She's good," I said, unsure why I was lying. Did she not know? I supposed it hadn't been big news to anyone but me when my mother died. Death was strange like that: it could change one person's entire world, but unless the news was spread by word of mouth, or through an obituary, or on social media, most people would never know. And my mother—who'd only ever played roles as extras and didn't keep in touch with anyone online or otherwise—certainly didn't make any headlines. Her death was silent.

Theresa tapped around her cheekbone with a finger, as though gently moving it into place. "Not acting anymore, I take it?"

"No," I said, "not acting."

Theresa nodded. "Probably for the best. She wasn't really any good at it."

This was news to me. To hear my mother speak, you'd think that whereas others were born to eat, shit, and sleep, my mother was born to act. "I once moved a dog to tears," she'd told me. "My emotional acting is so innate that even a dog, who can sense true inner feeling, believed my grief." My mother was certain that other people, who did not have this gift, were jealous. Maybe Theresa's envy had lasted over a decade.

"That's true," I said. In order to draw out what Theresa really thought, I couldn't get defensive, or else she'd revert to flattering pleasantries. I had to agree with her, to tarnish my mother's name for the sake of learning more about her. I set a lure: "She switched into a field more fit for her talents."

"Writing!" said Theresa. "I knew it. She was always better at making things up with her mind than bringing them to life with her body, if you know what I mean."

"Right you are again," I said, thinking of the last words my mother wrote: "Forgive Me." As enigmatic now as ever.

"Did she ever put on that play she was working on?"

"No," I said, truthfully this time. "She didn't."

Theresa shook her head. She looked a lot like my mother when she did that, her hair obscuring the sides of her face, allowing for a small window that was all sensory: eyes, nose, and lips.

"It was good, but I bet she wanted to play The Woman—and there's no way she could have carried a one-woman show."

With friends like these, I thought, no wonder my mother wanted to distance herself from others. I felt insulted on her behalf and guilty for playing along with kneecapping her memory. "Well," I said, "at least she had a sense of self-worth."

Theresa didn't notice the past tense. "Self-worth," she scoffed. "A pauper's pennies."

She scraped her chair back, as though to leave, but instead went to order another drink at the bar. She returned with two more G&Ts in her right hand and two shots cradled in her left.

"To foolish dreamers," she said, handing me a shot. Though she was at least twenty years my senior, she had a youthful vigor that I'd lost in my weeks haunting LA. After she slung back her Jim Beam, she smiled and said, "Much better."

She propped her elbows up on the table and leaned her cheek into her palm, looking at me without a word. The alcohol having done its job of finally putting her at ease, she said, "You know, you're kinda my type."

After several rounds of drinks, I returned with Theresa to her studio apartment in a squat two-story complex. The one other time I'd stripped completely naked in front of other people (even with my teenage hookups I kept some clothing on, afraid of the vulnerability of complete nudity) was when my mother took me to a jjimjilbang. I was fourteen or so, and had just shot up about four inches, newly embroiled in a war of attrition with the edges of tables and legs of chairs. But it wasn't just the Monet of bruises across my body that bothered me about being naked: it was also that I was too thin (this being just before the age where I regularly hit the gym and devoured calories like a manic chicken). Any baby fat I'd had was transferred into height and the tendons in the backs of my knees stuck out like sails. I was so thin that you'd lose me if I turned sideways.

In the steamy, single-sex wet room of the jjimjilbang, I quickly rinsed off while sitting on a plastic stool that had touched hundreds of butts before mine, though none quite so bony. Out of the corner of my eyes, I watched men of all designs lumber about without shame—hairy men, muscular men, overweight men—none of whom could have been my father since they were Asian, but still, I watched them scrub their backs with pink hand towels and scratch their asses. Out there in the city, they were working-class people of color, ground down daily to capitalistic dust—but here they were kings of their own plastic stool thrones. I tried to match their swagger, puffing up my chest and pooching out my stomach a bit, expelling grunts of contentment from time to time. That day I learned a valuable lesson about how to act like a man.

Now I had a body no one would be ashamed of, but over the past ten years I had only considered what others might think of it when I had clothes on. So as Theresa removed my shirt and jeans, I saw what she saw through the light of the streetlamp directly outside her window: a muscular chest, though with scant chest hair and mostly ringed around the nipples (which I normally would've plucked, but in the winter months I didn't take on any jobs that required me to be shirtless); my stomach a touch softer than I would've liked (and cutting me open would reveal an ode to the LA immigrant's gastronomical hustle tamales and tortas and char siu baos); and my knees, no longer knobby knockers, were now padded by muscular quads and calves. My ankles were a bit too delicate for my liking, but there was nothing I could do about that. She stopped before removing my boxers, and then it was my turn to repeat this ritual undressing on her. I started by unbuttoning her blouse, one loose button on its last thread. She was too drunk to notice when I tore it off.

Theresa's breasts were perfect mounds of silicone, which I hadn't encountered before. As her thighs squeezed my waist, fingers digging into the nape of my neck, her breath soured with alcohol, I emptied my mind. Strangely, this was easier if I looked at Theresa's face: here was a face I could touch with my fingers—sparse brows, a full lip, powdered cheeks obscuring all moles and marks.

"Are you on birth control?" I asked.

"Oh honey," she muttered into my chest. "I'm on menopause."

I couldn't remember how sex had felt when I was younger, but I knew that this was different. Back then it'd been a way for me to grip, thrust, and explode—giving me control over another body when I felt I had no control over my own. But now I was letting go; I wanted to be obliterated. I bit back a moan as she took me in and rocked me to a rhythm as innate as a heartbeat. She, however, was less circumspect about vocalizing how she felt.

She called me little boy, big man, handsome, kiddo, daddy, and I became a blank page for her to write all these identities onto. I had no words and no thoughts. I was nothing and no one. I was all desire. I embraced the void.

When it was over, I felt nauseated, but also raw: emptied and clearheaded in a way I hadn't been in days, months, maybe years.

As we lay in a tangle of damp sheets, she asked if I'd read my mother's play. I told her, honest at last, that I hadn't. There was a pause long enough that I thought she'd fallen asleep, but when I turned to look, her eyes were wide open, staring at the ceiling.

"Do you want to know what it was about?" she said, her voice scratchy from alcohol and the vocal exertions of the last twenty minutes.

What more did I want to know about my mother? I knew she was a hard worker with a nearly impossible dream, an aspiring actress—lovely, lonely, hungry. Theresa had added a few more characteristics to the list: bad actress and good writer, which meant that my mother was either a liar or delusional. I didn't like that. I didn't like it at all. I didn't like it because I already knew it. After all, who had heard her reciting lines more than I? My mother was no great actress, but so what? She hadn't been a great mother either.

"No," I said.

Unsure whether the fatigue that sideswiped me was from sex or the weight of acknowledgment, I understood, in the way that bones know when they break, that I didn't need to ask Theresa for any memories of my mother. I already had the information I needed. I'd known it this whole time. After all, why had I clung so fervently to this idea of redemption through the Rental Stranger business? Was it to follow in my mother's footsteps as an actor? To make other people happy? To pretend to be good so I wouldn't be my genuine, horrible self? To redeem myself for driving Mother to suicide?

The truth was more complicated than that.

I saw it clearly now. I was never bad, at least not worse than most people (and I'd met my fair share of people), but after my mother's death, I'd begun revising the story of my teenage years—casting myself as the villain who drove his own mother to suicide—not because it was true, but because that was the only way I could claim to have played any major role in her life. My cavorting around town had only ever been a desperate bid for her attention: for her to look at me, look for me. I thought that if

I couldn't make her happy, then I could at least make her miserable. And yet, whether I was at my best or my worst, to my mother I was never consequential enough to be a savior or a villain, only ever a side character. Every time she looked disappointed on those days I'd come home late after skipping school, or when she'd caught me sneaking a girl into our apartment, the barely contained disgust on her face wasn't for me: it was for herself. She'd had so many dreams, and she was achieving none of them. And on that day in late spring, when the failures overwhelmed her bruised and battered ego, she made a decision. If the world refused to acknowledge her, she would no longer acknowledge the world. Knowing that she would never get the role in this life that she felt she deserved, she wrote herself out of the script.

She was rapacious in her striving, which is how I knew (had secretly always known) where I stood with her: it was indifference, plain and simple. She didn't care about me. And all I'd wanted my whole life was to pretend that she had.

I could see now how I'd lived the years since my mother's death as a charade within a charade. There was nothing I needed to atone for, no need for redemption. I hadn't caused my mother's death—it had been her choice. I had barely factored into it. I'd made it all up in my head so that I could tell myself that I'd mattered.

"You're not curious?" Theresa said.

Maybe my mother had known this—that at her core she could care for no one but herself, and as her final act she wanted me to know it as well. I thought about her last words: not spoken, but written. Something to remember her by, something that might redeem her to a son who she did think about at least briefly in the final hours of her life—enough to push pen to paper one last time.

"I forgive her," I said.

"Oh," said Theresa, "so you did read it after all."

When she fell asleep—with a thunderous and divorce-worthy snore—I looked around the cramped apartment tinted orange by the streetlamp outside: stacks of scripts strewn everywhere, half-finished plates of food, pieces of sturdy furniture that seemed beyond her means (probably bought before the divorce) shoved up against each other. Theresa had mentioned that one thing she disliked about being divorced was waking up alone in the mornings. If I stayed the night, she could wake up to another person in her bed. We could exchange glances through sleep-filled eyes, happy dreams still playing at the edges of our lips. We could hold each other, pressed chest to chest. We could pretend that we were not lonely. It would be so easy to fake contentment.

Theresa didn't stir when I slipped out of bed. I took my time pulling on my shirt, boxers, and jeans; it was an any-man outfit that said everything and nothing about who I was.

As I let myself out into the cool LA night, a young Black woman in a bomber jacket walked by with her German shepherd, its teeth slick with saliva. I thought about sharks and daggers, and the answer to the riddle my mother had posed suddenly seemed obvious, as though illuminated by the headlights of the cars rolling by: I would stab myself to save the lives of those I loved. Maybe that was what love was—the willingness to sacrifice for others. Would my mother have sacrificed herself for me? Had she?

CHAPTER 31

By the time I arrived back at my place, it was well after midnight. I looked around the sparse living room, empty except for a futon couch and a coffee table with scuffed plastic edges. I'd placed the cartography case on top of the table, untouched but prominent, heavy and mournful as a tombstone. I opened it up. There was space inside for a piece of paper, a note, a final message.

I slipped out a sheet of paper from my backpack and began writing a letter to Lily, but the paragraph became a page, and the page became a chapter, and soon it was four in the morning. Though I had a contentious history with writers, I was beginning to understand their compulsion to write. The orderly march of characters across the page was an illusion of sense and meaning in the same vein as my job when I played a role for my clients (an exercise in one of several possible narratives that could, at best, brush its fingertips against reality) and yet: when my role was finished, or when the pen's ink dried on paper, reality shifted. Here, in writing, was a story of a man who tried but failed to run from his problems, for misery clung like a shadow to those who were afraid of the dark. Was he me? He was a version of me: one that might be understandable, if not to others, then at least to myself.

I could see Lily now, three hours ahead in New York City, waking up and trudging to the dining table to eat breakfast. Had she cried herself to sleep the night before? No, her eyes were not swollen; they were focused, looking at someone, Michael perhaps, who was sitting at the table in the spot where I normally sat. Or maybe she was looking at her mother, who was smiling, eating the omelets that Michael had prepared—slightly overcooked, just the way she liked her eggs. Lily was a bright girl; she saw how much happier her mom was, how the furrows that seemed a permanent feature on Mari's forehead were smoothed out now, relaxed by love. And in the lull of that calm, Lily would realize what she perhaps had always known, that her mom had never really loved her dad—needed him, yes, wanted him to save her, sure, but loved, no. Likely not. And the permanent strain in their household—some odd darkness that seemed always to creep in—was now somehow banished. That's not to say she wasn't angry; she was. She was furious and lonely, and she missed her dad, and wanted answers, but a small part of her also felt relieved. Hopeful, even. The way I felt after my mother died. I'd forgotten that part. Had my mother known that I'd feel that way? Maybe, one morning, she'd opened the freezer and recognized my face in the fearful expression frozen onto that crystalized mouse—the creature that she'd kept away from its natural course, now forever shielding its eyes, never to find grace in repose—and she'd realized that the best thing she could do, the only way we cursed individuals could make other people happy, was to leave. Or maybe that was an excuse to avoid the difficult, self-sacrificing work of loving.

I'd written to the bottom of my last sheet of paper. I flipped through the pages of my story, knowing that I would need more words—though how many exactly, I wasn't sure. But what I was sure of was that I couldn't really leave Lily, not yet. Because one afternoon, a package would arrive on Lily and Mari's doorstep, addressed not to Mari, but to Lily (deliveries to their household were rare, and packages addressed to Lily, unheard of). Both Lily and Piri would be in the apartment finishing their homework when the shipment arrived. Lily might hesitate and want to wait for her mom to come home before opening the box, but Piri would urge her to open it, and when she grabbed the kitchen shears and carefully (always carefully—her Christmas gifts were degloved so neatly you could wrap a new gift with the peeled sleeve) cut the seams of the cardboard box, lifting the flaps open, both of them would gasp at the shining metallic case inside with its worn engravings and brass clasps. They'd open it on the dinged dining table and a few sheets of paper would flutter with the disturbance. Lily, always drawn to words, would pick up the pages and begin reading while Piri oohed and aahed over the pointy dividers and ornate compass. Lily would know immediately who this gift was from, and her innate curiosity would compel her to read, despite whatever Mari might've said about her no-good, absentee father. She would read and read, reading me into existence.

My shoulders cramped from hunching over the low coffee table. After rolling out the cricks in my shoulders, I lay down on the couch, exhausted. I would buy more paper in the morning and perhaps another pen.

The cartography case waited patiently on the table.

In a few hours, the post office would open, and it would be open again tomorrow, and the day after, and the day after. Suffused in the glow of those days to come, I switched off the living room light, pitching the room to blackness and seeing, at last, that I cast no shadows in the dark.

ACKNOWLEDGMENTS

For all the love, encouragement, belief, and shoulder rubs—Jason Samuel Xie, thank you for just being a rock. Stranger would not exist without you.

Thanks also to Eric Simonoff, Criss Moon, and Caitlin Mahony at WME, who are the best champions anyone could ask for. And to Kara Watson, Sabrina Pyun, Dan Cuddy, Stephanie Evans, Jaya Miceli, Kassandra Rhoads, and Brianna Yamashita and the team at Scribner, infinite gratitude for bringing this book to life!

A special shout-out to Diana McKeage, my big ol' word nerd friend who is as brilliant as she is generous. I think I'm finally becoming less allergic to commas thanks to you.

To my Write or Die—Aviva Mandell Shabtai, Honor Vincent, Jason W. Short, and Warren Woodrich Pettine—you've been with me from my first-ever writing workshop (NYU's SPS!) to now, and I can't wait to continue to learn, write, and eat more raspberries with you all.

ACKNOWLEDGMENTS

I'm continually grateful for the friends and mentors whose hands, visible or invisible, have helped shape these pages: Laura Venita Green, Brooke Davis, Lin King, Cameron Menchel, Sam Lipsyte, Weike Wang, Kristopher Jansma, Gabriel Bump, Ben Marcus, Heidi Julavits, Elissa Schappell, and Joshua Furst.

Growing up, I always thought that being a teacher was the toughest job in the world because it was the most important. I still believe that. Thank you to the K–12 teachers who've encouraged me to be my best from a young age: Ms. Scadina (5th grade), Mr. Russell (7–8th grade math), Mrs. Moore (11th grade, AP Lang), Mr. Phipps (11th grade, AP USH), and "Madame" Patricia Wilson Caine (9–11th grade, French . . . duh).

To all my friends who have encouraged me and believed in me through my pivot from lawyer to writer—thank you, thank you, thank you.

And to my nonhuman companions: Momo, the little white dog who was with me at the beginning of this journey, and Juno, the not-so-little white cat who is here now.

Finally, the biggest of thank-yous to Mom, Dad, Alex, and Fiona— what a blessing it is to be a part of a five-star family.